Really-Truly Stories

Really-Truly Stories

Volume
4

Gwendolyn Lampshire Hayden

Pacific Press®
Publishing Association

Nampa, Idaho | Oshawa, Ontario, Canada
www.pacificpress.com

Illustrated by Vernon Nye

Revised ed. Copyright © 1983 by Pacific Press® Publishing Association
Printed in the United States of America
All rights reserved

You can obtain additional copies of this book by calling toll-free
1-800-765-6955 or by visiting http://www.adventistbookcenter.com.

ISBN 978-0-8163-6289-9

February 2017

Contents

1

Tree-house Tricksters

"SAY, Jesse, is it true that you and Dick are going to enter the school's pet contest?"

Jesse looked up quickly as Willie questioned him concerning the much-talked-about event soon to be held in the Condon school.

"I should say we are. Aren't you and Ralph?" Jesse replied with enthusiasm. "In fact, we're already counting our chickens before they're hatched."

"Chickens? *What* chickens?" Willie asked. He wrinkled his smooth brow in a puzzled frown. "I don't think you folks have any extra-special chickens good enough to put in a pet show. Why, you've just got plain old Rhode Island Reds, the same as we have. And neither Ralph nor I would think of taking them to school and entering them in the contest. People would think we were crazy!"

"Well, maybe they would. But they won't think we're crazy. Neither will you and Ralph when you see the two white Leghorns that we're buying from Fry's poultry farm."

"Fry's poultry farm?" repeated Willie in astonishment. "Why, those chickens are the most expensive in Lane County. How can you afford to buy any of them?"

"Oh, we've saved up every penny we could, and with some help from Dad we've finally got enough money to buy a young hen and a rooster. We'll get them some time this week, just as soon as we finish the special cage we're making for them. Then we'll feed and take care of them for the next few weeks and get them as tame as possible. We've got plans for showing them off—and, well—I think we'll be sure to win the blue ribbon.

"After that, we're going to save enough eggs for a hatching and go in the blue-ribbon chicken business."

"Sounds good," grunted Ralph, kicking his black laced shoes against the tall weeds that bordered the dusty hillside path. "But right now I'm not one bit interested in blue-ribbon chickens. What I'm hungry for is a good big stew with dumplings. Yum! It makes my mouth water to think how good those last eggs tasted—the ones we got from Dick Reed's poultry house."

"They sure did!" laughed Jesse. "That reminds me! Whose turn is it to furnish the main dish for our next campfire feed at our tree house? Is it yours, boys?"

"Not ours," they chorused, and Willie continued, "I think it's Benny Reed's turn, but I'm not sure. You know we always try to keep our turn secret, so none of us will know exactly what to expect.

"But we'll sure have to make big plans for this feed. After all, a Presidential election comes only once every four years. And this year we've promised ourselves a real celebration, especially if Woodrow Wilson's elected our next President."

"Woodrow Wilson!" exclaimed Dick. "Who cares who's elected! We're all too young to vote, so what difference does it make to us who's going to be our next President? All I care about is the food we're to have for supper that night."

"You're too little to know what you're talking about," Willie answered with the superiority of his extra two years. "But my dad says it *will* make a lot of difference to the country as to who's elected President. You know my dad came to America from a foreign land when he was a young man, and since then he's always tried to read and study about our Government. He says we've got the best nation on earth, and we should appreciate it. He talks to us a lot about such things—I guess that's why Ralph and I get such good grades in United States government and history."

"Well, what he says may be true enough," Dick granted grudgingly. "But I'm still going to be powerful hungry that night, regardless of who's President. Hadn't we better begin making our plans? What are we supposed to take, Jesse? Potatoes and onions for a stew?"

The four schoolmates sauntered idly on over the hilltop, chattering busily about the next month's tree-house celebration. And in their excited discussion no further mention of the school pet contest was made.

"Don't you think we'll win the prize, Jesse?" Dick asked anxiously several weeks later as they stood admiringly in front of the big cage that securely housed their two beautiful white Leghorn chickens. The boys laughed aloud at the answering caw, caw, caw, from the cage and reached through the barred door to stroke their chickens' shining white feathers.

"There. How's that for an answer?" Jesse joked gleefully. "Our rooster says, 'Of course we'll win.' And somehow I really think they will, Dick. Why, they've gotten so tame we'll be able to drive them right across the school stage. Every time we've practiced with their little harnesses they've done better and better. Now they're almost perfect.

"Of course, I don't know how they'll act when we get them up there in front of a big crowd, but we'll just have to take that chance."

"They behave much better right now than Benny's chipmunk or Harold's pet snake. Besides, their feathers are so snowy white and their combs are so red that they look just grand. Oh, I can hardly wait for the pet show," Dick concluded breathlessly.

"Say, there's one thing we must be sure to do. Mother said we could have some of that red, white, and blue ribbon she saved from Fourth of July celebration," Jesse interrupted quickly. "I'm going to make some reins with them, instead of using that old cord we've been practicing with every day."

"Red, white, and blue ribbons?" questioned puzzled Dick. "What do you want to use those for? It's long past the Fourth of July. It's almost November, or didn't you know that?"

"Of course I know the date. I'm not that stupid," retorted Jesse. "But since the pet show comes the day after election, I'm going to be patriotic and make our chickens look as patriotic as I can. It'll be a good idea, and it's one that might help us to win the prize. Everyone'll be so excited about the new President that, no matter who wins, we'll still be all right."

"Say, you've really got that figured out!" Dick exclaimed. For once he looked at his older brother with actual admiration for this undoubted stroke of genius.

"What do you say we go and get those ribbons right now! I'd like to bring them out here and hold them up against our chickens. Those bright colors are going to look mighty nice against their shiny white feathers."

"No sooner said than done," Jesse agreed, and for some time the boys stood admiring the effect of the long colored streamers against their pet chickens' dazzling-white coats. It was not until their mother's "O boys, I need two buckets of water brought from the spring," that they tore themselves temporarily away from the poultry cage and its inmates. Even as they carried the brimming buckets they continued to talk about the coveted prize they were sure they would win.

All too slowly the days crawled along, until the morning of election dawned bright and clear. Jesse and Dick didn't wait to be called, but jumped shiveringly out of bed and hurried down the narrow stairway into the comfort of the hot kitchen.

"Hurry and wash, boys," urged Mother. She gestured toward the wash bench with its gray granite pan and big cake of Fairy soap. "I just put clean towels there and some washcloths too. Be sure to wash your necks and behind your ears. You can't see the back of your heads, but everyone else can. And clean your fingernails. There's enough dirt under them to start a fall garden."

"That's right," added Harvey. "You shouldn't go to school with dirty fingernails. Nice boys don't."

Jesse bit back the "Oh, be quiet!" that almost spoke itself as he saw his Aunt Rhoda look reprovingly at his older brother.

"Thee should not tease thy younger brother, Harvey," she said in her soft Quaker voice. "It is not kind of thee to do so. Thy own hands were none too clean when coming down to breakfast. Didn't thy mother ask thee to wash also?"

Jesse almost whooped with delight at the sight of his brother's reddened cheeks and embarrassed silence. He wished that kind Aunt Rhoda would visit them for a long, long time before she returned to her home in Kansas.

"All right, boys," Mother urged. "Let's sit down so that your father can say the blessing. He has to leave within the next twenty minutes, or he won't get to work on time. It's six-fifty now. The sourdough biscuits are light and fluffy, and I made an extra panful so that you could eat your fill. Please hurry."

Jesse and Dick bent their close-cropped heads while their father said the usual blessing. Then they quickly filled their plates with the steaming hot fried potatoes, eggs, and buttered biscuits covered with delicious apple and quince jam.

"M-m-m, but that tasted good," sighed Dick as he pushed back his twice-emptied plate with a sigh of utter contentment. "I sure wish I could eat some more, but

I just can't. But if any biscuits are left, I'll take them along with us tonight when we have our tree-house potluck supper."

"That's right!" exclaimed Mother. "I hadn't remembered that this was the time for your club celebration. We've been so busy thinking about election day and tomorrow's pet show at school that I'd forgotten all about your supper with the boys. What's on your club agenda tonight?

"I suppose you'll have a lot of fun discussing the Presidential candidates: William Howard Taft, Teddy Roosevelt, and Woodrow Wilson. My, but you boys certainly have been excited about this election."

"Wouldst thou that thy Aunt Rhoda made an apple-sauce and nut cake for thee?" offered their kind aunt, smiling at these young nephews whom she had journeyed so far to see. "I would be glad to bake something for thee and for thy friends."

"Say, that's a fine idea," nodded Dick. "We usually just take what we can find in our pantries, but since this is election day, maybe we should have something extra special. Thank you, Aunt Rhoda. We'd like to have one of your good cakes."

"But we'll like that good stew with dumplings even better," asserted Jesse. The two boys hurried out to the chicken pen to feed and water their two pets.

"I wonder what the folks would think if they knew how we got our main dish for each club supper?" Dick asked curiously, as he stared at his rooster's bright, beady eyes and proudly arched neck. "What do you suppose Dad'd say?"

"What would he say? You mean what would he *do*, don't you?" Jesse responded. He patted the seat of his trousers as though even then he had experienced his father's direct action as a reply to Dick's question.

"He'd thrash the daylights out of us, so don't you be a baby and go and tell him. We'll shut you out of the tree-house club if you do, so just remember what I've said."

"But—but isn't it stealing?" Dick questioned worriedly. He felt his conscience troubling him as a result of his last Sabbath school lesson at the little Fairmount church.

"Isn't *what* stealing?" Jesse answered absently, surveying his hen with gloating pride.

"Why, to go out and take vegetables and eggs from our neighbors whenever we have a feed. My Sabbath school teacher said that it was wrong to take anything that belonged to another person, and so I think this must be stealing."

"Oh, Dick!" Jesse retorted quickly. He spoke louder than usual, as though the volume of his tone could cover up his own secret misgivings about the club plan. "You know as well as I do that we never take any supplies from any families except the ones who live right here in our own neighborhood. The last time we went over to Reed's place we got a sack half-full of potatoes and carrots for a stew and several dozen eggs for an omelet, and I don't think Mr. Reed even missed them. He must have a hundred laying hens."

"Well, he did miss them," Dick said firmly, "because I heard him talking to Mrs. Reed one day when I went down to play with Benny. He got real mad and shook his fist in the air. He yelled, 'Take some of my best hatching eggs, will they? I'd like to catch those pesky nest raiders. I'd give them something to remember.' "

"He must have wanted to show off," Jesse added. "He's really pretty good-natured. But we'll have to be more careful, or we'll get caught. I'm glad it won't be our turn again for a while. Somebody else'll have to go out and get the eggs tonight. All we'll have to take are some potatoes and onions and the cake Aunt Rhoda's going to bake for us."

All day the boys kept thinking of the good tree-house supper planned for that very evening. They knew it would be a delightful prelude to the next day's pet show at school, when they were certain to win the blue-ribbon award for their two beautiful chickens.

"I just know we'll win," Jesse asserted for the hundredth time, as he and Dick finished caring for their two pets and, supplies in hand, headed across the sunset-tinted hill toward the big tree house.

"We'll feed our chickens again the first thing in the morning," Jesse continued. "Then we'll have time to brush their feathers after we take them to school. They'll get all mussed up in those gunny sacks we've got to carry them in, but that can't be helped. That's the only way we can get them there.

"Say, there are some of the fellows now. Harvey's there too, and it looks as if they're getting ready for a game of run, sheep, run. Let's hurry up so we can play. Last time we had to build the campfire and help cook, but today we don't have to work.

"Come on. They're going to choose sides. Hurry!"

Until long after dark Jesse and Dick ran back and forth across the hilltops and into the fir forest that bordered Reed's pastureland. The campfire had been glowing for hours before the last of the weary stragglers sank to the ground beneath the tree house. They all sniffed hungrily at the mouth-watering smells that poured out from the big black kettle hung over the bright red embers.

"M-mm. Stew and dumplings. And fried potatoes and onions with eggs. And roasted apples. Who could want anything better than this?" grinned Jesse. He refilled his hastily emptied plate and licked his fingers preparatory to picking up another tasty bit of well-baked apple. He stared across from him at Benny, who sat busily eating, with his legs straight out in front of him, exposing to view the worn and patched soles of his high-topped shoes.

"This sure tastes good and no mistake," agreed Willie. "We hit on the right idea when we let our folks provide tree-house dinners for us."

"I should think they'd get suspicious after a while and wonder what was happening," added Benny's visiting cousin. He was uneasy about the way the boys excused their practices.

"Oh, our folks have lost so many young pullets that they don't miss a few eggs now and then," Jesse explained. "Sometimes skunks raid the henhouses, or sometimes eagles swoop down and grab a squawking hen. So the folks just blame the varmints whenever another chicken's missing or whenever a few eggs are gone.

"We're always mighty careful to be real quiet when we sneak into the henhouses, too. If we don't raise a disturbance, no one else ever knows about it," he added. "And this way it doesn't cost us anything. We couldn't afford to have these good suppers out here if we had to go to the store and buy our food. Besides, I don't think we're really stealing, because we don't take food from anyone but our own families."

Soon the boys carefully put out the campfire, gathered up their various belongings, and called a cheer-ful good night as they disappeared homeward in the darkness.

The next morning Jesse and Dick hurried out to the chicken house, gunny sacks in hand, ready to take their prized chickens to the school pet show.

"I'm really getting excited, Dick. Aren't you?" queried Jesse excitedly as they neared the big pen. "I just know we're going to win. I've seen many of the pets that the boys are going to take to school. But none of them can compare with ours. Our chickens are really beauties.

"Have you got the red, white, and blue ribbons to put on them? We mustn't forget those. We'll find out this morning whether Woodrow Wilson was elected President, and we'll need those ribbons."

"Yes, I've got them," Dick answered, patting his hip pocket. "And they're all folded up neat and nice. Aunt Rhoda fixed them for me and put them in a paper sack. Yep. They're in my pocket, all right."

"Here we are," Jesse said importantly, trembling with eagerness now that the time had come to enter their beautiful white Leghorns in the contest. "I'll go around the cage and reach in and get the rooster and hand him to you and then——"

He stopped short while a puzzled look crossed his face. Hastily he bent and looked in the cage. "Why—where—they're gone, Dick; our chickens are gone!" Jesse exclaimed. His ruddy cheeks paled with anxiety.

"What do you suppose—do you think Dad could have let them out?"

"No, he wouldn't do that," Dick asserted. "He knew that we always kept them shut up so nothing could happen to them. I know he wouldn't turn them loose. And neither would Mother nor Aunt Rhoda."

"Well, how about Harvey and Lee? I wouldn't put it past either of them to do a trick like that," Jesse said fiercely. "I'll just bet they did."

"But they couldn't have," Dick answered quickly, almost in tears over this unexpected disaster. "Lee stayed down at Lottie's. Don't you remember that he wasn't going to come home at all last night? Mother wanted him to help sister. He was going to chop up the wood she'd ordered. And Harvey was with us all evening. No, they couldn't have done it either.

"Neither could Thelma. She's too little to reach up to the cage handle," Dick said slowly, making no effort to cover his dismay.

"Then who *did?*" Jesse asked, his voice thick with disappointment. "Somebody's let them out, and we probably won't be able to catch them in time for the school pet show. I'm just sure some of the neighborhood boys were here. I——"

"I think they were, too," Dick interrupted. "In fact, I *know* they were. At least, one was. Look down there, will you?"

Jesse looked at Dick in surprise as his younger brother squatted on his haunches and pointed toward two footprints sunk deep into the half-dried mud close beside the watering trough. His heart sank despairingly as his eyes followed Dick's pointing finger to the telltale marks.

"Now do you see what I mean?" Dick spoke grimly. "I'm afraid that we'll never see those chickens again. All we've got left is the cage—and those red, white, and blue ribbons!"

"You mean—oh!" Jesse exploded. "I know what you mean. Someone sneaked down here in the dark while the rest of us were playing. When he began looking for eggs he opened up this cage, too. Now our prize chickens are gone.

"You're right, Dick. We'll not find our white Leghorns in time to enter them in the pet contest today, because we're already late for school right now. Those chickens are probably having a fine time eating bugs out in the forest back of our house, unless a hungry hawk has eaten them.

"And Ben's the one who let them loose, too, because these are his footprints. Don't you remember seeing those funny-looking patches on the soles of his shoes? He sat right across the campfire from me, and I remember looking at them.

"Just you wait until I tell Dad what's happened. That hen and rooster cost a lot of money. They weren't just plain, ordinary chickens, no siree!"

"I don't know how you're going to tell him," Dick answered dryly. "After all, we've taken eggs from Reed's henhouse. It was all just a part of our neighborhood game. If you tell Dad that Benny Reed took our eggs, you'll have to tell him that we took Mr. Reed's eggs. I don't think that's going to sound—or feel—very good. Do you?"

As Jesse looked into Dick's straightforward stare he seemed to see mirrored there the words his younger brother had quoted only the day before: "My Sabbath school teacher said that it was wrong to take anything that belonged to another person, and so I think it must be stealing when we rob a neighbor's henhouse."

For an instant he looked before he blinked his eyes and sniffed audibly. "I—I guess you're right, Dick. And I guess you were right when you said it *was* really stealing. Somehow our potluck meals at the tree house just seemed like a lot of fun before this happened. But now that our pet chickens are gone, somehow those stolen suppers don't seem like such a good idea any more.

"From now on we're going to bring our share of the food from our own home. And I'm going to ask the other fellows to do the same.

"I, for one, am not going to vote for any more 'free' meals. I think they've proved to be pretty expensive ones, after all."

2

The Unloaded Gun

I WISH I had a gun of my own," Jesse grumbled. He dumped his armload of fir wood into the big kitchen wood box and turned toward his younger brother Dick. "I don't think it's fair for dad to let Lee have a .22 rifle when we can't have a gun. After all, Lee's not much older than I am. And he's as stingy as he can be about lending his precious gun too. He never lets me practice shooting."

"Then he's doing exactly what I told him," spoke Dad Hayden from the bottom of the basement steps. "Furthermore, I'll take the .22 away from him if he disobeys me. I've taught him how to shoot, and I've showed him how to unload and clean the gun. Then I've taught him to hang the unloaded gun in its proper place on the gunrack.

"After all, Jesse, you have no cause to complain. Lee's six years older than you. When you're his age I'll get

a gun for you and teach you how to shoot. Until then you are to leave the gun alone!"

"Why—I didn't know you were home, Dad," Jesse gasped. "Did you get through work early today? Dick and I came home from school just a few minutes ago, but we didn't expect you until six o'clock."

"Yes, I can see that you weren't expecting me." As Jesse heard his father reply he glanced at him quickly and was relieved to see the familar good-natured twinkle in his brown eyes. "We quit work about two o'clock today, but I stopped downtown to attend to some business. Then I did a little marketing for your mother. We're getting low on a few of our supplies, so I ordered six hundred pounds of flour and twenty cases of canned goods. As soon as the fall rains begin the grocery wagon won't be able to drive in on this dirt road.

"It pays to have everything on hand when winter comes—food in the pantry and the storeroom, canned fruit on the fruit shelves, and a basement full of wood. I like to have everything attended to, especially now that your mother's not feeling well. She needs all the rest possible."

"Just what *is* wrong with Mamma, Dad?" Jesse asked. He swallowed hard against the lump that always came into his throat whenever he thought of his mother's failing health. "We thought she'd get better right away as soon as we came up here from California, but—well —somehow she looks thinner every day. I don't think it did her any good to move here, do you?"

"I don't know, son. I don't know," Jesse heard his father's tired sigh. "All we can do is to hope and pray that this mild, damp climate will be the thing that will restore her to health. She's happy here, at least, so for that reason I'm glad we made the move. We all liked living in California, but after your sister Lottie married and moved to the Willamette Valley your mother wanted to be near her.

"If you boys will only stop your arguing, you'll do much toward helping your mother get the necessary rest and quiet. I know you boys mean no harm, but you'll just have to be more thoughtful. If you want to argue, do so when you're playing back in the woods with Ralph and Willie. Mother can't hear your noise from that distance."

"All right, Dad, we'll try to be quiet " Jesse agreed soberly, while Dick nodded his close-cropped head and stared at his dusty feet. "We try to be still, but then something happens or Lee and Harvey tease us or Thelma tags along when we want to play, or———"

"I know. I know all about it, son," nodded Dad Hayden. "I was a boy once upon a time too, you know. And I liked to play just as well as you. That reminds me. I saw the Paasche boys on my way up the hill, and they asked if you could play for an hour before supper. I said I thought you could. They're probably on their way here right now."

"Say, thanks, Dad," grinned Jesse. "Come on, Dick. Let's meet Willie and Ralph down by the gate. Then we'll go back and have a game of fir cones with them. They beat us last time. Let's see if we can't win today."

The four playmates ran to the towering fir woods a block or so back of the hillside acres that Dad Hayden had purchased soon after the family's arrival in Oregon. They quickly lost themselves behind the huge tree trunks and peeked out now and then to bombard each other with their hastily gathered fir cone ammunition.

"Ouch!" yelled Dick. "Ralph banged one right against my ear. Ow! Help me get him, Jesse. Come on over here and help me hit him."

"There!" shouted Jesse. I'll pay him back. I got him. I got him that time. Come on, Ralph and Willie. We won. Game's over."

Laughing and puffing, the four friends threw themselves headlong on the grass and rolled over and over in the cool green ferns that carpeted the forest floor. Content to rest quietly for a few moments, they clasped their hands under their heads and stared dizzily up, up into the distant tops of the trees swaying against the blue sky.

"Look at that chipmunk," Dick whispered. "See? He's right over my head."

"And there's another one," Ralph answered in a low voice.

"Say! Look at that blue jay. He's a saucy fellow," Jesse added.

"It's all right to be talking about blue jays and chipmunks," Willie added somewhat scornfully, "but I saw something really interesting the last time I came back here. Right over there in that little grove were three deer. They were almost near enough to reach out and touch. My, what a shot they'd have made for some hunter."

"Deer? And you saw them last week?" Jesse asked. He sat up so quickly that the friendly little chipmunks dashed up the trees and the blue jays sounded their harsh cries and flew away.

"That's right," Willie nodded. "I s'pose folks are hunting back in the woods and have scared them down close to town. There'll probably be lots of deer around here now until hunting season's over."

"I'd sure like to see those deer," Jesse said wistfully. "Of course, I couldn't shoot them, but I'd like to see them just the same."

"You couldn't shoot them?" asked Willie curiously. "Why not, I'd like to know?"

"Oh, dad doesn't like to have the wild creatures shot," Jesse explained. "He says he likes to look out and see them on the place. He tries to make friends with them. Why, right now he's got a pet squirrel that comes to the kitchen door. And there's a woodpecker who knocks on the front porch every morning and waits for dad to throw out some crumbs. Anyway, even if he'd let me, I couldn't shoot anything. I don't have a gun."

"No, and he can't use Lee's either," spoke Dick, with all the irritating wisdom of a younger brother. "Dad said he wasn't even to touch Lee's gun."

"Do you mean you can't practice with Lee's .22—a great big boy like you?" Willie asked.

"That's right. I can't," Jesse added, his cheeks flush-ing under Willie's mocking gaze. "Of course, you're older, and you could go ahead, but I don't dare."

"Well, I'm glad my dad isn't so strict," Ralph chimed in proudly. "I'll bet I could practice with Willie's rifle if he had one."

"Oh, so that's what you think, is it?" Willie laughed

and grabbed Ralph's arm, ready for a tussle. In the friendly scuffle no further mention was made of the gun, and in the busy hours that followed it was forgotten.

Jesse and Dick thought that food had never tasted so good as did supper that evening. Before grace was said they stared hungrily at the mound of fluffy mashed potatoes, the bowl of rich gravy, the steaming stewed tomatoes and green peppers, and the tempting dessert of chocolate cake and yellow peaches served with thick clotted cream.

"Yumm—mm, but that was good," Jesse said as he fell back against his chair and looked at his empty plate. "Too bad Lee and Harvey weren't here to help out with all this food. I ate until I'm about to burst."

"Well, son, the best remedy for that condition is a little exercise," smiled gentle mother. "I'll let you and Dick carry out the dishes."

"Yes, and wash and dry them too," added Dad Hayden. "I want your mother to lie down awhile. You're both good kitchen help, so we'll turn the rest of the evening chores over to you."

With practiced hands Jesse and Dick began scraping, stacking, and carrying out the plates. Then, while Dick built up the fire in the big black kitchen stove, Jesse carefully carried the steaming teakettle over to the sink and half-filled the two gray granite dishpans.

"While I wash the glasses you'd better get the kerosene can and fill the lamps, Dick," Jesse said. "It'll soon be dark enough to light them. Then after we're through here we'll have to carry the water buckets up to the spring to fill them."

"I don't see why we have to do all that tonight," whined Dick. "I'm tired. Besides, there's enough water to last until morning."

"No, there isn't," answered practical Jesse. By the time I refill the teakettle and the stove reservoir so mother'll have bath water there won't be a drop in those big buckets, and you know it.

"Now don't complain. We always have to do our chores as soon as we come home from school. Just because dad let us go and play awhile tonight is no sign that he didn't expect us to do our work before bedtime."

"Oh. I suppose so. But just the same, I get awfully tired of lugging water and wood and cleaning old sooty lamp chimneys," grumbled Dick, with his lower lip drooping disgustedly. "Sometimes I wish we'd never moved from our old home. Why, we had electric lights and running water in the house down there. Up here we live like pioneers."

"Well, I think it's fun," stoutly asserted Jesse. "And you do too, most of the time. Anyway, you know as well as I do that we came here for mamma's health. And you couldn't expect dad to spend all the money he had just on a house downtown. He bought these three acres and built this place so that we'd have a nice home someday. Just wait until all those cherry and walnut trees that we set out are grown. We'll really make some money then."

"Oh, pooh!" grumbled Dick, picking up the dish towel. "I'll be an old man by that time, all bent over and worn out from work. Come on. Let's hurry and finish these dishes."

The kitchen lamps were lighted before the last of

the dishes were dried and put away, and the mellow light from their frosted glass chimneys shone gently into the corners of the room. It glinted upon the big stove's bright brass trimmings and upon a long slender object leaning against the wall near the kitchen door.

Jesse's brown eyes widened as he watched this object, and he pursed his lips in a long whistle. Quickly he glanced over his shoulder as he hurried toward the door and leaned over the forbidden object.

"What—say, Lee's left his gun out here!" exclaimed Dick, watching his brother. "What do you know about that! That's the first time he's ever done such a thing. He must have been out practicing on his target near the berry patch and then come in and put his .22 in the corner after he finished unloading and cleaning it.

"He really must have left in a hurry or he'd have hung it on the gunrack. Dad would really scold Lee if he knew he hadn't put his gun away."

"I know he would!" nodded Jesse. He'd probably tell him he couldn't use it for a long time." He wrinkled his forehead as he stood and looked at the shining .22. Then he turned quickly toward Dick. "I'm going to put Lee's gun on the gunrack. Then dad'll never know Lee forgot it and left it here," he said quickly. "That way he won't get punished, and he can go on practicing on his rifle range."

"You hadn't better!" warned Dick. "You know good and well dad told you never to touch that gun. You'll get a good whipping if he catches you."

As he heard Dick's warning words Jesse felt his heart plunge down toward his boots. But then, like a whisper,

came the voices of Willie and Ralph as they had talked
that afternoon in the woods.

"You mean you can't even practice with Lee's .22?
A great big boy like you?"

"Well, I'm glad *my* dad isn't so strict. I'll bet I could
practice with Willie's rifle if he had one."

As he thought of his own longing to learn to shoot,
Jesse felt his heart fill with self-pity. A bitter taste welled
into his mouth as discontent flooded through him and
turned his happy mood into one of gloom.

"Oh, dad'll never know unless you want to be a
tattletale and tell him," Jesse answered sharply. He
grabbed the coveted rifle and cradled it lovingly in his
hands. "Besides, I'm only going to put it away. What
are you afraid of? It's unloaded, so it's perfectly safe.
It really is a beauty, isn't it! I'd give just about anything
for a .22 like this.

"Wouldn't it be fun to target practice like Lee does?
Now this is the way I'd do it. Let me show you, Dick.
You stand still and pretend you're the target. First, I'll
aim this at your head, like this. Then I'll aim it at your
heart. And then I'll aim it straight at your knees. So!"

And carried away by his game of make-believe, Jesse
sighted down the shining rifle barrel and pulled the
trigger of the unloaded gun.

Bang!

"Ow, Ow! Oh, my leg. My leg. I'm shot. You've
shot me with Lee's .22. Dad! Dad! Jesse's shot me!"
wailed Dick as he fell to the floor.

Jesse reeled backward, almost overcome by the gun's
loud, unexpected explosion and by Dick's frantic cries.

He stared wildly from the smoking gun to his younger brother's bleeding leg. All during his father's and mother's hurried entrance into the kitchen and the examination of the gunshot wound he felt frozen with fear. It was not until his father came hurriedly up to him that he aroused from his shock and sprang into action.

"You'll have to run down over the hill to the store telephone and call the doctor, Jesse." Through the dull roaring in his ears he heard his father's voice. It sounded to him as though it came from far, far away.

"Hurry. That's a bad wound. The bullet's gone in at the kneecap and come out at the thigh. Dick may lose a lot of blood. Run as fast as you can, and tell Doc Bartle we need him mighty bad."

All during the following nightmarish hours Jesse felt that he would never again be able to laugh and play. His eyes burned as he watched his younger brother sink into an exhausted sleep, his bandaged leg stretched stiffly out on the bed. His throat ached as he saw his frail mother's tired face and his father's trembling hand patting her bowed shoulders. But it was not until his father spoke that the long-held-back tears filled Jesse's eyes and spilled down his freckled cheeks.

"I wish you'd give me a good licking. I deserve it, Dad. I know I do," he sobbed. "I told Dick I was just going to put Lee's gun back on the gunrack so that you'd never know Lee had forgotten it. But that was only an excuse.

"But honest, Dad, I thought it was unloaded. I didn't know it had any bullets in it. I'd never have pointed that rifle at Dick if I'd known Lee had forgotten to unload it. We knew you'd always told him never to leave a loaded gun around the house. And so—and so I—just picked it up and——"

As he listened to his father's reply Jesse put his aching head against Dad Hayden's broad chest and sobbed as though his heart would break.

"No, I'm not going to punish you, son," he heard his father say wearily. "I think you've been punished enough already. And your punishment will continue for some time, for you'll not only have your own chores to do but Dick's as well.

"When he gets cross and tired of being an invalid it'll be up to you to amuse him and think of games to help occupy his time. Mother'll be down in bed for days as a result of the shock she's suffered. That means that you and I'll have to do most of the housework and cook-ing, for Thelma's too little to be of much help. There'll be no more playtime for you for a good many weeks.

"Lee will have to help too, for he's really more to blame than you," Jesse heard his father continue. "He should never have left the gun there in the first place— and especially a loaded gun. He's older than you boys, and he should realize the responsibility that falls upon anyone who owns a rifle.

"But we should all be thankful to God for sparing Dick's life. Just think what might have happened had you pulled the trigger while the gun was pointed at Dick's head."

Jesse shuddered. He wondered what had kept his hand from pulling the trigger as he sighted along the gun's shining deadly barrel straight into his brother's eyes.

"I think you've learned a lesson tonight that will stay with you through life, son," concluded Dad Hayden. "Just remember, it is easy to do the wrong thing, but it takes real courage to do what is right.

"Anyone can be disobedient. But if you will only remember that disobedience leads to sorrow and suffering, not only for yourself but for all those around you, you will never again be found guilty of shooting an unloaded gun."

Jesse never forgot the trust in his father's eyes as he replied, "I know what you mean, Dad, and from now on I'm going to try to do the right thing."

3

Cache in the Cabin

MY, BUT IT feels good to be up and around again after so many days in bed," Dick said. He skipped back and forth on the leaf-scattered path under the big oak tree.

"I sure got enough rest to last me a lifetime. Why, I was in that old bedroom long enough to grow a whole new leg!" He and Jesse laughed heartily at the thought of such an impossibility, and then turned quickly at a loud halloo down the road.

"Halloo yourself!" yelled Jesse. "Hurry up, Willie and Ralph. Let's have a game of fir cones back in the woods."

"I shouldn't think you'd want to go back in the woods," puffed Ralph. He sounded out of breath from the steep climb up past the shady oaks toward the wide porch. "The last time you went back there was the day you shot Dick. Maybe you'll have some more bad luck if you go there again."

"Well, I'm not superstitious, boys," Jesse said. His merry face sobered for a moment. "I brought all that bad luck on myself, and I don't intend to do anything as foolish as that ever again.

"Now, we'd like to go out and have some fun. Mother said we could. Dick's been up and around a few days, but he hasn't really had a chance to work off all that extra pep, and neither have I. All I've done for the past six weeks is housework and dishes. All I know any more is the broom and mop. I don't know whether I'll be able to recognize fir trees or not." The boys laughed merrily as they ran toward the nearby woods.

"Whenever I get back in here I like to pretend I'm really a pioneer or a frontiersman like Daniel Boone. Don't you?" questioned Jesse, his brown eyes alight with interest. "I wish I'd lived in those times, so I could have gone out into the wilderness and laid claim to new lands. Our history class has been studying about Colonial days in America. Our teacher's going to give a prize to the one who makes the best report on 'My Most Interesting Discovery.' "

"Well, you can go West to make your discovery, can't you?" asked practical Dick. "That's what all the pioneer stories say—'Go West, young man, go West!' "

"Go West?" repeated amused Willie, grinning at Jesse over the heads of the younger boys. "Why, how much farther West could you go? You don't want to jump off into the ocean and stake out a sea-bottom claim, do you? After all, the Willamette Valley's only eighty miles from the Pacific. Didn't you know that?"

"Oh, I guess I did," disgruntled Dick said shortly.

"But I keep forgetting. It always seems to me as if we're just about living like pioneers up here."

"We're far from it," Jesse disagreed. "But I'd give a lot to make a really exciting discovery just once. At school we read about discovering new lands and new people. I'd like to discover something new!"

"I don't think there's much chance of that," Ralph added, tossing his blond curls back from his forehead. "We've covered every inch of this ground dozens of times. Why, we could find our way around here blindfolded. I know we could."

"Say, that's a clever idea for a game," Jesse exclaimed. "Let's try it. What do you say? We've never done that before."

"Try what?" Willie inquired eagerly. "Now what's your idea?"

"Why, just this. Now listen everybody, and I'll explain."

Jesse saw that the blue jays, woodpeckers, and squirrels peered curiously down from the high safety of their fir branches at the four heads pressed close together. He knew that they wondered what to expect next from these strange two-legged creatures who came so often to their own particular woodland.

"All ready," Jesse shouted. "Keep your eyes closed tight. We haven't got any blindfolds with us, so you'll just have to promise not to look even once.

"Now. When I give the signal we'll all whirl around three times, and then we'll start out in the direction we're facing when we stop. But don't open your eyes until you bump into something. We'll see if we can't be real explorers today and discover something new. Ready. And no fair peeking."

"But can't we look even once?" questioned Dick. "S'pose I run smack into a tree? I'm not anxious to skin the end of my nose."

"Sure, you can look when you hit something," Jesse replied. "But the fun in this game of explorer will be to keep walking with your eyes closed. That way you can try to find some path or some spot that we haven't seen before."

"Can't be done, my boy. Can't be done," Ralph shook his head. "As I said before, we've been here too often."

"Well, we can give it a try," Jesse grinned. "Now! On your mark. Get set, and—go-o-o-o-o!"

Round and round the four boys whirled, and then with close-shut eyes and outstretched hands they began groping forward, east, north, and south. Slowly they moved in the unfamiliar darkness of their closed eyelids, stepping cautiously over ground that now seemed unfamiliar to their stumbling feet.

"Ouch!" muttered Jesse as he bumped headlong into another boyish figure.

"Ouch yourself!" he heard Dick reply. "Watch where—oh, I forgot. Yes, I've got my eyes shut too."

"Then keep them that way," Jesse replied tartly. "I'm going to start off to the side. Both of us can't go neck and neck along this narrow trail."

Even before he finished speaking he began moving away from the sound of his brother's voice. And soon he felt, from the very silence of the forest around him, that he was deep within its green heart. Cautiously he advanced westward, still keeping his eyes shut tight, still holding his arms straight before him lest he crash into one of the great trees that now surrounded him on all sides.

And then it happened, so suddenly that he had no chance to save himself from falling. Jesse felt his foot catch on some strange object. Then he fell flat upon his face on the mossy ground.

"Whew! That was quick!" he thought wryly. He pushed himself up from his prone position and blinked his eyes against the light that momentarily dazzled him. "What—oh, it's a root from that big tree. Well, at least I didn't bump into anything. I wonder how I happened to fall over that. I don't remember seeing this place before, and we've played back here dozens of times. Hmm! I wonder where I am?"

Jesse ran his hand over his close-cropped head and stared wonderingly around the little glade into which he had accidentally stumbled. His eyes widened, and his mouth rounded in a loud Oh as he looked toward the right.

"It's—but it can't be!" he exclaimed. "I must be dreaming. Maybe if I pinch myself, I'll wake up. Ouch! No, I'm awake all right. But how—when—where in the world did that cabin come from? It—why, it's so old it looks as though it'd fall down any minute."

He stared unbelievingly at the gray, weathered log cabin. There it stood behind the interlacing tree branches that drooped over its rotting roof and slanting walls. Jesse saw that it was almost hidden from sight.

"A cabin!" he repeated. "A real honest-to-goodness pioneer cabin. I'm going to peek inside and see if there's anything there."

Cautiously he sidled up to the rough walls, looking behind him nervously at every other step. He felt as though unseen eyes were peering at him from the green-walled circle of the little hidden forest glade. Then, taking a deep breath, he pulled back one of the sagging window shutters. Screwing up his courage, he looked quickly through the opening into the interior of the cabin.

Unbelievingly he stared along the bright shaft of sunlight that shone into the one big room and lighted up the great fireplace at one end. Wonderingly his eyes darted the length of the room and toward the loft above, and then back once more to the blackened hearth.

"It is! It really is a pioneer cabin. Why, it must be. There's a spinning wheel just like the one we saw in our history book, there's the old-fashioned long-handled spider that the folks used for cooking their food in the fireplace, and there's even a funny old built-in bed at the other end. Maybe there's something else upstairs too. I'm going to see."

But as he hurried toward the heavy door he stopped and shook his head. "No," he thought, "it wouldn't be fair for me to go in alone and look around. We promised each other that if we found anything, we'd let the others know. I guess no one else has found anything exciting. But I certainly have, so I'd better give the signal and get the boys here. Then we'll do some exploring all together."

Jesse put his two fingers in his mouth and blew three shrill, piercing blasts that set the quiet forest echoes fleeing. He listened for a moment before he repeated his signal, and then nodded his head as far, far away he heard one, two, three code replies.

"They're on their way right this minute," he thought gleefully. "Now let's see if they stumble onto this place the way I did. I don't think they will, because their eyes will be wide open. I'd never have found this hidden glade if I hadn't had my eyes shut tight. Pretty soon I'll whistle once more to give them a better clue to my hiding place. Then I'll just wait quietly here and see if they can find me."

And grinning mischievously, Jesse sat down on the cool ground and listened to the crashing sounds that echoed through the woods as his playmates followed his whistle, floundering along in their haste to find him. He chuckled to himself as he heard their excited voices and smiled broadly when they came close enough so that he could understand what they were saying.

"But he must be here. We all heard him whistle!"

"Yes, but *where* is he? We've looked and looked and *looked*, and still we haven't found him anywhere."

"Do you suppose something could have happened to him? Maybe there are bears back in here. After all, sometimes we've heard cougars screaming at night. Perhaps he bumped into a bear—or—or——"

As Jesse heard his brother's worried voice he knew that it was time to reveal his hiding place. Putting his fingers into his mouth, he again gave the piercing whistle that was the despair of his quiet-loving mother.

"There he is!" he heard Dick scream. "He's right here somewhere. Come on, boys. Begin looking all over again." Around and around the outer edge of the little glade the boys ran, increasingly puzzled by the unseen nearness of their adventure-loving companion.

"Jesse. *Jesse!* Where *are* you?" he heard Willie yell.

"Right here," he called through the thick, tangled growth that masked the secret forest nook. "Go past that big-topped tree, and then get down on your hands and knees. You'll see an old path there. Look close. It's almost covered up by ferns. There's a big root sticking out of the ground right by the entrance. I fell over it, and that's how I found this place."

"Well, what do you know about that?" Jesse heard the boys exclaim. "We've walked by that old root lots and lots of times, but we certainly didn't know there was a hidden path there."

"And just look. Here's a regular little clearing 'way back in here. Say, this makes us feel like real explorers!" added Willie.

"Yes, and you'll feel even more like explorers when you look into that cabin over there," Jesse said quickly. He pointed toward his prize discovery with all the pride of a Columbus sighting a new land.

"A cabin! A real cabin!" shrieked the boys. Then, with Jesse in the lead, they ran pell-mell toward the log house.

"Now just a minute!" Jesse warned as they stopped short at the door. "When we go in let's be careful and not tear up things. Maybe we'll find something really interesting if we look carefully."

For several moments only the sound of the boys' quick breathing broke the long-undisturbed silence of the old cabin. Carefully they moved across the splintered floor, peering into the blackened mouth of the yawning fireplace and staring at the worn old spinning wheel that had stood mute and forsaken for so many years. Carefully they took turns climbing up the rude ladder that led to the sleeping loft, only to find it empty, save for a thrifty squirrel's carefully gathered store of winter nuts.

At last Dick spoke. "Well, I guess that's all. It really is an old cabin. But there doesn't seem to be anything here except a spinning wheel and that funny-looking old frying pan. I think we'd better be going. It must be getting late."

"I guess you're right," Jesse nodded, looking in surprise at the sun's slanting rays. "I'd hoped we'd find something really exciting here, but there doesn't seem to be anything out of the ordinary. So we might as well go home. We can come back some other day."

His heavy shoes resounded against the wood with a sharp cr-rr-ack as he jumped from the loft ladder to the worn floor. He gave a muffled cry as he felt his feet sink down through the broken boards and push against a hard object on the ground beneath.

"What—say, I've found something. I don't know what it is. But something's here," he exclaimed in surprise. "Do suppose——"

Jesse left his unanswered question hanging in midair as he climbed gingerly out of the hole and knelt at the edge of the broken boards.

"What is it? Let's have a look," Ralph urged. "Move over so we can see too, can't you?" Impatiently he shoved Jesse.

"Now just a minute. Who fell through the floor anyway? Let *me* have a look," Jesse said half-angrily. "Here. Let's pull this rotten board away. It's no good any more."

The four boys yanked and tugged at the flooring until a large space lay exposed. Quickly they bent down and stared at an irregular mound almost hidden beneath a pile of leaves and dirt.

"Watch out!" quickly warned Willie as Jesse stretched out an exploring hand. "There might be snakes or rats or something there that'd bite you. It doesn't pay to take any chances."

"You're right!" Jesse agreed. He snatched back his hand as though it had already been bitten to the bone. "Look, Dick. Hand me that stick. I'll drag it through these leaves. Maybe——"

The boys almost stopped breathing as Jesse poked and prodded gently with his weathered stick. They expelled their breath in one great collective sigh of disappointment as he uncovered the leaves and disclosed a small box of carefully wrapped food and milk.

"It's only food," almost wailed Dick. "I thought we'd found some real treasure. And besides, if there's food there it shows that someone else knows about this place too. So it isn't an old deserted pioneer cabin, after all."

"I call it a dirty shame," groaned Ralph. "It looked as though nobody'd been here for years and years. But now that we've found this box it sort of spoils things."

"Oh, I don't know," Jesse said stoutly. He tried to speak bravely to cover up his own disappointment. "Perhaps—well, look. Those cans have been here a long, long time, I'd say, because they're awfully rusty along the outer edges. Maybe we've still found a place that's been forgotten. And besides, we can always use food for our tree-house suppers—— as long as it isn't Blue Ribbon chicken!

"Here, Willie. Help me lift this old box out of the hole, will you? I just wonder——"

"Yep! I think I'm right! Dick, I need that stick once more. I want to try something." Jesse spoke hurriedly.

Carefully he scraped away at the ground while the puzzled boys watched him in wonderment. They gasped as his stick suddenly plunged through the apparently hard crust, and they all leaned close to the edge when he began enlarging the small opening that he had made.

"Now what do you think you've found?" Willie asked quickly. "Is there something more?"

"I—I think so," Jesse answered quickly, almost choking in his excitement. "You see, I figured that if this was a good hiding place for one person, it must have been a good hiding place for another person. Maybe some pioneer who lived here hid something in that hole, and then forgot it or went away or died. After a while the dirt and leaves covered the place. Then later someone else came here and used it for his secret storage place too.

"There! I struck something, all right. Help me, fellows. There's a little box of some kind there. I'll try to dig it out. Wait. Careful now!" Fairly trembling with eagerness to see what lay under its bent lid, the excited boys knelt around the tiny faded tin chest that Jesse carefully lifted from its forgotten hiding place.

"C-c-can you open it, Jesse?" stammered Dick. "D-d-do you s'pose it's locked? Oh, wouldn't it be awful if it wouldn't open!"

"It's locked, all right," Jesse answered through clenched teeth. "But I think I can pry it open." He pulled and twisted at the rusty lock.

"There! I've got it! And just look at that, will you?" He pulled the little treasure chest toward him and bent his head for a closer look.

"What is it, Jesse? What have you found? Let me see too," begged Dick, tugging at his brother's coat sleeve.

"Just a minute," Jesse replied. He gently lifted a small object and held it before their wondering eyes. "Here's a little locket with an old faded picture inside. And here's a pretty gold pin with a black border, and—say, look at that old-fashioned necklace with the dark-red stones. What do you suppose they are? They must really be old. I never saw anything like that before."

"Those are garnets," Willie answered while the boys gaped at him in utter amazement that he should know so much about jewels. "I know, because my great-aunt had some just like them. She had a gold pin almost like that one too."

"I wouldn't be surprised if they weren't worth a lot of money, Jesse. What are you going to do with all these things you've found?"

"Do with them?" echoed Jesse, parrotlike. "Why, I—I don't know. I've just found them, and beyond that I haven't thought."

"Well, you can't leave them here," Willie said firmly. "After all, if we—or you—found this place, someone else will be sure to find it sometime. And they'll also do some exploring. So you hadn't better leave those things here for somebody else to take."

"I guess I hadn't better," Jesse said slowly. "I'll tell you what I'll do. I'll take them with me and give them to dad. He'll know what should be done with them."

"Come on, boys. It'll be dark before we get home if we don't hurry. Here. Let's put this food box and flooring back in place. If no one claims it, we'll come back someday and have a royal feast. But right now let's head for home as fast as we can."

With excited whoops the boys left the little clearing and started across the wooded hills. But though he ran as fast as the others, Jesse kept careful hold on the little old-fashioned treasure box that he had unearthed from beneath the cabin's plank floor.

"Just a minute," said Dad Hayden as four eager voices tried to explain at one time just what had happened. "Let Jesse tell me about the box and the old cabin. Maybe I can get it straight if I listen to one of you at a time."

The boys looked knowingly at one another as they heard Jesse's voice flow on and on and saw Dad Hayden's look of rising interest. They felt sure that something unusual was about to happen, and at Mr. Hayden's first words they knew they would not be disappointed.

"Looks as though you've really made an interesting discovery, Jesse," Dad Hayden said as soon as Jesse finished telling all about the game of blindfold and his accidental discovery of the deserted cabin. "What would you say about it, Mr. Thompson? Did you ever hear of this place?"

The boys felt their hearts almost leap with excitement as they heard their old neighbor's reply and watched his nod.

"Yes, I remember hearing my wife tell about some folks that settled here in the early days. They stayed out there for some time, and then all at once they left. One of the family became ill, and for some reason they went away in a hurry. As far as I know, none of them ever came back again.

"My wife's been dead for a good many years, and I'd forgotten all about the story until now. But it's very likely that those folks left the few treasures they had in what they thought would be a safe place. They probably planned to return. But their precious possessions have lain right there all this time."

"But who could have left that canned food in the same hole?" questioned Jesse. "If all that happened a long time ago, it must have been before tin cans had been invented. Who could have left it there?"

"That's easier to answer," smiled the neighbor. "I imagine that some solitary woodcutter used to hide away a few canned supplies. Then when he worked 'way back there in those woods he'd have plenty to eat should he decide to spend a few days in the old cabin he'd found. Remember, it's only been in recent years that there's been any kind of road at all back as far as your house. And it's not a very good one, even yet. At the time the cabin was built this area was wild and wooded."

"Yes, and it's still like that where we were today," nodded Dick. "I don't see how Jesse ever found that place. I really don't."

"Well, he made an interesting find, I must say," smiled mother. "Son, you did right to bring the little treasures home, and not leave them there. Perhaps we can find the owner."

"Yes, I'll go to the bank tomorrow," nodded Dad Hayden. "The bank officials may be able to trace the owner of these articles. Some relative would be very happy to recover the family keepsakes—especially this necklace. It really is beautiful, and I would say it had considerable value."

"You'll probably get a reward, Jesse," smiled old Mr. Thompson. "After all, you'd be entitled to something for such a find. I know I'd be very glad to reward an honest boy who found my family keepsakes."

Jesse leaned back against his straight chair with a sigh of utter bliss as he heard Mr. Thompson's words. "Well," he replied, "I don't care so much about the reward. I didn't bring the little tin chest because I thought I'd get anything.

"But what I am excited about is finding it. Just wait until I tell my history class and my teacher about my discovery. Maybe I'll be the one to win the history prize for 'My Most Interesting Discovery'! I can hardly wait to see their faces when I tell them about the cache in the cabin."

4

Badger-hole Boa

HURRY, girls! It's time for you to saddle your horses and start out. I don't want the cattle to stray too far away from the river."

As she heard Papa's deep voice calling them, Myrtle wrinkled her forehead in a cross little frown.

"Oh, dear," she sighed. "I'd hoped that just for once we wouldn't have to ride after our livestock. They're such stupid creatures. Why can't they be content to stay nearby instead of roaming across the plains?"

"You know the answer as well as I do," replied younger sister Louise. "They have to find food, and so of course they must keep moving along. But Papa never lets them go too far away, and after they make a wide circle out on the prairie they'll come right back here again."

"Well, I'm always glad when they return," replied Myrtle. "In fact, I wish they were here right now, so we could stay near the house, and play with our dolls."

"Maybe we can still have fun," Louise said cheerfully. "Remember that we won't be out on the prairie today. We'll be a couple of miles away, that's true. But we'll be near the river and right beside the deep bank that slants down toward the water.

"That's my favorite spot. Maybe we'll have time to dig down into one of the badger holes on top and see if it comes out in the riverbank. Wouldn't it be exciting to find some baby badgers?"

"I don't think we'll find any at this time of year," laughed Myrtle. "And you'd probably never find any, for badgers are too sly to be caught out of their burrows in daylight. Or if we saw one, we might not recognize him. Papa says a badger can roll up into a ball and lie so motionless that he becomes part of the landscape.

"But you're right about one thing anyhow. We can have lots of fun there. Shep always likes that place too. He enjoys digging down into the prairie dog and badger holes on the prairie. Remember the time he unearthed a rattlesnake? He was certainly surprised!"

"Come on. Our horses are ready, and it's about time for Papa to call us again. We'll hurry along so we'll have time to play awhile on the riverbank. Let's not forget our lunches, though. We'll be really hungry by noon, and we'll be too far away to make an extra trip home."

As Myrtle and Louise rode across the prairie they looked at each other with sparkling eyes. It seemed to them that every journey through the waving, rippling grasses brought new sights and new sounds. They thought that even the familiar cheery call of the bobolink sounded more beautiful than ever in the clear sunlight.

"My, but this cool water feels good," Myrtle sighed happily several hours later as she sat at the river's edge and splashed her bare feet up and down in the stream.

"I think we've watched the cattle long enough," she continued. "Surely they can't stray very far while we sit here and eat our lunch. M-m-m. These bean sandwiches taste delicious. Mamma's certainly a good cook."

"She surely is," agreed Louise. "And I'm almost starved. I was ready to eat an hour ago. Let's just take our time. Shep can watch the cattle as well as we can. I'll send him out there right now.

"Here, Shep. Come on, boy. Here, Shep! Come here." But though Louise called and whistled and called again she heard no answering bark from their faithful dog.

"Why, he was here just a few minutes ago," said Myrtle quickly. "He can't be very far away. I'll—listen! It sounds as though he's snarling at something. What do you suppose it could be?" Her eyes widened as she heard the dog's distant growls.

"Oh, nothing very much," Louise answered gaily. "He's probably sniffing down a badger hole. And no doubt the badger's gone out the rear entrance and is laughing at him from a safe distance. Call him again."

"Shep! Come here, boy. Come here right now." Myrtle called again and again. But though the girls heard Shep's snarls and growls draw nearer and nearer, still no dog appeared.

"I can't understand Shep's acting like this," Myrtle said in a worried voice. "He's always come whenever we've called him. Do you suppose he's caught in a trap of some kind?"

"I don't see how he could be," quavered Louise. "But if he is, we'll have to get him out. And I-I'm scared. I just know something's wrong or he'd be here right now."

Gr-rrr!

Myrtle and Louise looked at each other's white faces and saw fear mirrored in each other's frightened eyes.

Gr-r-r-rr-r.

They heard Shep's growls rise to a sharp crescendo and then break into a series of wild barks that splintered the noon's calm stillness.

"He's found something!" gasped Myrtle. "Oh, what is it? He's never acted this way when he's found a badger or a rabbit. Maybe——"

The girls clung to each other in terror as their dog's pain-filled cry burst full against their eardrums. They stared in horror as the rolling body of Shep cascaded down the steep bank. They watched fearfully as the dog clung to a huge, loathsome object into which he had sunk his sharp teeth.

"*Oh!* OH! OH!" screamed Louise. "What is it?"

"It—it's a snake," cried Myrtle.

"A snake!" wailed Louise. She burst into frightened tears as she clung tightly to her sister's neck. "It can't be! Who ever saw a snake as big as that?

"Why, it must be twelve feet long! It can't be a real live snake. We're dreaming, and it's a nightmare. That's what it is."

"I wish that was all it was," Myrtle answered grimly. "But we're wide awake, and so's that snake. Look! Poor old Shep's let go, and now he's darting in again to try to get a strangle hold.

"Quick! We've got to help Shep or he'll be killed. Let's grab our horsewhips. They're good and stout. We'll have to use them on the snake. Maybe we can wear it down so that Shep can finish the job.

"Hurry up. It's now or never."

The trembling girls advanced cautiously toward the huge reptile and the wildly excited dog. Bravely they called to their pet as they watched for an opportunity to strike at the snake's flat, darting head.

"There!" yelled Louise. "I hit him. Now you hit him, Myrtle. Hit him hard or he'll kill Shep."

"Watch out!" warned Myrtle. "He sees us. Maybe he'll start after us. Hang on, Shep. Hang on, old boy. We'll help you."

The girls felt hot perspiration trickle down into their eyes, but so precious was every second that they dared not relax their guard.

Hit! Slash! Jump forward! Jump back! Hit! Slash! Hit!

"Oh, I can't lift my whip one more time," groaned Louise. "I—I can't."

"Quick!" commanded Myrtle. "You've—got to. We'd —never be able—to run—to our horses—now. That snake'd—get us—sure. He's—angry!

"Hit him again. Hit hard. There! That's it."

Again and again they slashed at the writhing coils. Again and again the faithful dog strove for a death grip on the back of the snake's evil head.

At last as tired, battered Shep feebly worried the back of the dead snake, the exhausted girls sank to the ground and burst into tears.

"It—it's dead," sobbed Louise. "And I'm crying because I'm glad."

"So am I," choked Myrtle. "I thought for a while that good old Shep was done for and that we were too. If it hadn't been for him, we might have been killed. Why, that awful snake was right up there at the top of the bank all the time. We'd have gone there as soon as we'd finished our lunch."

"Good Shep," quavered Louise. "Come here, good dog. There, there, old fellow. It's all you can do to walk, isn't it? Well, you can ride home with me if you want to. And I'm about ready to go right now."

"I am too," nodded Myrtle, blinking her tear-filled eyes and pushing back her wind-blown hair. "But we'd better wait awhile. Papa wouldn't like it if we left the cattle too early in the day. And we're safe now that that awful thing's dead."

"Well, I still don't want to look at it," sniffed Louise. "Let's get our horses and ride out on the prairie. I'll feel a lot safer there than I do here.

"Come on, Shep. We'll go slow. That's a good dog."

All afternoon the girls could think and talk of nothing but their terrible adventure with the huge snake that had so nearly killed faithful Shep. All afternoon they could scarcely wait to get home and tell Papa and Mamma all about the most terrifying event of their young lives.

But a few straying cattle delayed them, so that it was past sunset when they rode into the dusty barnyard and dismounted stiffly before the barn door. They whirled at the sound of Papa's sharp inquiring voice.

"Where in the world have you girls been? You've always been as punctual as the clock itself. But this one time when I needed you to help me with some extra chores you've dawdled along the way. It's almost an hour past time for you to be home. What have you been doing?"

Louise and Myrtle looked at each other and wondered which one should tell Papa the almost unbelievable story of their narrow escape.

"Well, girls?" asked Papa. "Speak up. I'm waiting to hear what you've been doing. You know that Mamma and I expect you to be on time. And you always have been until now."

"It was a snake!" Louise and Myrtle both spoke at the same time and with such force that the word fairly leaped across the barnyard toward Papa.

"A snake!" exclaimed Papa. "Well, why be afraid of a little snake? You were safe enough on horseback, weren't you? I'm afraid that excuse isn't good enough."

"But, Papa, it wasn't a little snake. It was an enormous snake," gulped Louise. "It must have been twelve or fifteen feet long. And it——"

"Oh, come now, Louise," spoke Papa impatiently. "You surely can't expect me to believe that there are fifteen-foot snakes crawling over the Kansas plains. Why, you're old enough to know better. Such large reptiles live only in tropical countries, and Kansas certainly isn't a tropical land."

"Really, Papa, it *was* enormous," added Myrtle. "And it almost killed Shep. It might have killed us, too, if he hadn't fought it."

"Come, come, daughter," said Papa. "Has your imagination run away with you too? I must admit that Shep looks mighty bedraggled and as though he'd been in some kind of fight. But I can't accept that story of an attack by a huge snake. I'm more inclined to think he's been up to some mischief and you girls are defending him."

The girls were almost in tears at their father's apparent unwillingness to believe their story.

"Honestly, Papa, there really was one," gulped Louise. "And if you'd only go out there to the bend in the river, you'd see its dead body."

"Well, we'll see," said Papa kindly, though still unbelievingly. "We'll go out in the morning and find out what frightened you so much. I'm sure something must have happened to upset you this way, for you girls have always been very dependable."

Myrtle and Louise slept fitfully, for their slumbers were troubled with frightful dreams of their encounter with the snake. Several times they awoke with a start and could scarcely wait for dawn the following morning. As soon as they roused they crept achingly out of bed and dressed in their carefully laid-out clothes.

"I'm glad I have a clean gingham dress to put on," said Myrtle. "Ugh! I can hardly bear to touch those clothes I wore yesterday. Just as soon as we get back I'm going to get out the washtub and scrubboard and wash them. Mamma'll have the water kettles all filled and heating on the stove by the time we return."

"I'm glad, too," replied Louise, as she buttoned up her stiffly starched dress and started to brush and braid her long hair. "Of course we really didn't touch the snake, but just the thought of those awful coils still makes me feel dirty and dusty.

"I wonder what Papa'll think of our story when he gets out there and sees that snake? He'll be sorry then that he scolded us for being late."

"Why—what—my, oh, my!" was all that Papa could say as he sat on horseback on the high edge of the steep river bank. He stared down at the ugly, motionless body stretched full length near the water's edge.

The girls watched as he quickly dismounted and hurried down the slope. They saw his steps slow as he cautiously approached the lifeless body.

"It—why, girls, it's a boa constrictor. It can't be! But it is!" they heard him exclaim in awed tones. "It's a real boa constrictor. And to think that you two girls and old Shep fought this thing and killed it without any help from anyone. Why, it could easily have killed all of you. How did you do it?"

It was a proud moment for Myrtle and Louise.

"We prayed, Papa," Myrtle answered. "And then, while we were praying to ourselves, we took our buggy whips and fought the snake. We just couldn't desert Shep."

As Myrtle and Louise noted Papa's quick glance they saw that his eyes were shining with unshed tears.

"I've seen some strange sights in my lifetime," he added, as he climbed back up to his waiting horse, "but this beats them all. I can't understand how that boa could have gotten here. I'm going right now and get the townsfolk to come and see this snake.

"I'm going to bring Mamma, too. I want her as well as everyone else to know how brave you girls have been. And I want you to forgive me for doubting your word. You will, won't you, daughters?"

"Of course we will, Papa," both Myrtle and Louise answered quickly. They felt their throats choke up as Papa quite frankly wiped his eyes and asked their pardon.

Louise and Myrtle could scarcely wait to get home and look up information about the boa constrictor in their encyclopedia. Quickly they found the right page and began to read the description.

"The boa constrictor is a large snake of the tropical parts of America. It kills animals for food by squeezing them with its long body. It is not poisonous. Boa constrictors are between ten and fourteen feet long. . . .

"Boa constrictors defend themselves as other snakes do, by throwing their heads and the front part of their bodies at the enemy, or *striking*. Their teeth can make bad wounds, because they point inward. Boa constrictors cannot swallow horses, cattle, and other large animals . . . but they can swallow animals much larger than their heads, because the bones of their jaws can be stretched far apart. . . . This allows big things to pass into the throat and body, and these parts can also be stretched. Boa constrictors, like other snakes, can live many months without food.

"It feeds chiefly on small mammals and birds, seizing them with long needlelike teeth, and then wrapping itself around them and crushing them to a soft mass that it can swallow. . . . After a meal it goes into a heavy sleep, which sometimes lasts several weeks.

"It does not lay eggs. The young are born alive, like those of the higher animals. It may give birth to as many as fifty young at one time.

"Its color is ruddy brown, shading to deep red at the tail, with crossbands of tan, turning to a palish cream color toward the tail. . . . Its real name is constrictor constrictor."

"My," exclaimed Myrtle. "If I'd known all that I'd never have had the courage to fight that boa. Would you?"

"I guess not," Louise replied. "But it's a good thing we didn't. Otherwise, we wouldn't have saved good old Shep."

Myrtle and Louise never forgot the excitement aroused by the killing of the boa constrictor nor the many folks who dropped in to call upon them and hear from their own lips the story of that awful day. They were more than thankful for the information and the warning brought to them by one man who rode some distance to give them his solution to the mystery.

"I wanted to tell you girls that the boa constrictor you killed must have escaped from a circus train that was wrecked many miles from here about two years ago. All of the animals were captured except two boas. They got loose and were never found. No one will ever know how that snake could have gotten way over here nor how it kept alive during the long, cold winter months we have out here on the Kansas plains.

"Maybe it burrowed down into a badger or prairie dog hole, where it stayed snug and warm and feasted well on small animals and snakes. At any rate we know that it was very much alive when Shep found it and dragged it over the riverbank to you girls.

"However, what I wanted to tell you was this. As I rode over here I came by that same river bend. At first I thought my imagination was playing tricks on me. But as I neared that very spot my dog began barking wildly and running back and forth as though there was something dreadfully wrong. Though I called and called to him he paid no attention to my voice. He just kept on yelping in a queer high-pitched way that was unlike any noise he'd ever made before.

"Even though I was in a hurry I felt I should ride over to the riverbank and see just what was wrong. And as I got there I saw—or thought I saw—a huge head rear up and look at me from a big hole in the riverbank. Quick as a flash it disappeared as soon as it saw me. And, to tell the truth, I disappeared in the opposite direction just about as fast."

Myrtle and Louise laughed as he told of his flight.

"Now I think it's very likely that the mate of that dead boa constrictor is living out there near that same place. And I think anyone who goes there should be well armed and on the lookout. Of course, we'll organize a searching party, but I doubt that we'll find anything. After all, those two monsters have been loose for several years, and no one's seen them until now. It's lucky for all of us that one was discovered. It makes me shiver to think what might have happened if some small child had gone down to the river's edge."

"And it makes me shiver to think what might have happened to my girls," said Mamma shakily.

"That's right," answered Papa. "I certainly don't want you girls going back to that spot any more. Our neighbor's right. There just might be another snake there."

"Well, don't worry about Louise and me wanting to go there," Myrtle answered thankfully. "I'm sure that neither of us cares to ever again meet another badger-hole boa."

5

The Birthday Bear

NOTHING exciting ever happens to us," sighed Stephen. He threw down his animal adventure book and scowled in disgust. "I've just finished a really thrilling story about camping in Alaska. *Those* folks certainly had a grand time! But nothing like that ever happens to me!"

"What's this I hear?" Dad asked as he sank into the comfortable rocking chair by the fireplace. "Did you mention camping?"

"Did I! I certainly did," exclaimed Stephen. "And I'd give just about anything to be able to go somewhere right now. I'm getting mighty tired of staying home and working."

"Well, that's odd," smiled Dad. "How did you happen to be wanting a camping trip just at the very time I'd decided to take you on one?"

"Honest?" gasped Stephen. His brown eyes sparkled with excitement as he stared at his laughing father. "Are we really going right now—even before we finish the garage?"

"Yes, we're really going," nodded Dad, "although not right now. To tell the truth, I, too, am somewhat tired of work. Mother and I have talked over plans for your birthday, and we've decided that a family camping trip to Crater Lake would be a nice present for all of us. And since you and I share the same birthday, we'll be responsible for all the plans. What do you say?"

"I say Yes," cried Stephen. "And it'll be wonderful to see Crater Lake. Why, only last week we read about it in our geography lesson at school. It said that Crater Lake was one of the wonder spots of the world."

"That's true," nodded Dad. "It's been many years since I went there as a young boy. Roads in those days were rocky and unpaved, and it took much longer to make the journey than it does now. But the lake will be as beautiful as ever. It truly *is* one of the wonder spots of the earth.

"Now let's hurry along and drive a few more nails in that garage flooring. Later this afternoon we'll go downtown to one of the sporting goods stores and see what we can do about getting sleeping bags."

"Sleeping bags!" cried Stephen. "O Dad! Are we really going to buy some? Have we saved enough pennies and nickels for mine?"

"Yes, son, we have," smiled Dad. "We've been saving for a long time. Last night when Mother and I counted that jarful of pennies and buffalo nickels, we found enough there for two warm sleeping bags, one for you and one for Marilyn. That'll be a good start on our camping equipment. Mother and I can sleep in the car on this trip.

"We'll start all over again on our penny and nickel jar, and it won't be long before it'll be full once more. It seems to fill up quite rapidly when our small change isn't spent for ice cream and candy bars."

"Yes, and you said that now almost every nickel given you in change turned out to be a buffalo nickel!" laughed Stephen. "Let's hope we get lots more of them."

"Lots more of what?" questioned Marilyn from the doorway. "Food? You're always hungry, Steve."

"You'll be hungry, too, when you hear what we're going to take on our trip to Crater Lake——"

"Crater Lake! Are we going there?" Marilyn interrupted excitedly. "O Mother, just listen——"

"Yes, dear. I know all about it," nodded Mother. She joined the family group and smiled at each eager face. "Your father and I have invited Edwin Jess and Esther to go also. They'll leave baby Ricky in good care while they're away. It would be difficult to take him."

"I wish Ricky could go too," mourned Stephen. He was very proud of his year-old nephew and often served as baby sitter.

"He'll be better off at home where he can follow his usual schedule," Mother explained. "Besides, he might catch cold while we're camping up at the lake. The altitude there is high above sea level."

"Yes, and we might have to run from the bears," joked Dad.

"Bears!" gulped Stephen. "Do you mean we'll see real bears out in the woods?"

"Indeed we will," nodded Dad. "Furthermore, it'll behoove all of us to keep a safe distance from Mr. or

Mrs. Bruin. Those bears aren't to be trusted, even though they are accustomed to seeing people for five or six months of each year.

"In fact, we'll undoubtedly be handed a warning when we pay our one-dollar registration fee at the park entrance. This pamphlet will not only tell us about the natural beauties of this famous Government camp but it will also warn us to 'Beware! Do not feed the bears!' "

"You're right, Dad," said Stephen a few days later, as their heavily loaded car left the friendly ranger at the park entrance station. "This little booklet that he gave us tells all about the lake and surrounding country. It also warns us not to feed the bears."

"Br-r-r! Who'd want to?" shuddered Marilyn. "It gives me the cold chills just to think of seeing a wild bear out here. I'd probably fall in a faint if I met one face to face. I'm certainly not going out of my way to donate any food to the wild animal population of this park, not if I can help it."

"Pooh!" sniffed Stephen scornfully. "That sounds just like a girl. A bear wouldn't hurt you if you kept quiet and minded your own business, would he, Mother?"

"We won't argue the question," replied Mother. "But to be truthful, I don't know. I suppose that there are good bears and bad bears. We'll just be careful and obey all the park rules. I understand that there are many nice camping spots near Crater Lake Village. Surely we'll be quite safe there, as other people will be nearby. Many families visit the park during the year, and some of them stay for some time.

"While we're traveling," she continued, "shall we find out something further about Crater Lake National Park? Between our park bulletin and our travel books, we should become quite well informed. Sight-seeing is always much more interesting and rewarding if we know something about our subject."

"I think that's a fine idea," agreed Marilyn. "We'll really remember more about our trip if we read about the park beforehand. Then I'll be able to give a report in geography class this fall."

"You certainly will," agreed Mother. "We've already learned that 'the first white man to gaze upon one of earth's most beautiful lakes named it Deep Blue Lake. As he discovered its miraculous blueness deep in the crater of an extinct volcano he stood in silent awe.'

"Perhaps you'd like to read further in this description, Stephen," Mother concluded. "Begin right here at this paragraph."

" 'Crater Lake was discovered June 12, 1853, by John Wesley Hillman, a prospector hunting for game and gold,' " began Stephen. " 'Crater Lake National Park was created in 1902. It includes an area of 250.5 square miles on the crest of the Cascade range in southern Oregon. The unsurpassed feature of the park is the scenic beauty of Crater Lake, an exceptionally deep body of water cupped within the crater of an extinct volcano. The lake is famous for its ever-changing hues. . . . At times its surface is lashed into countless white-capped waves.

" 'The lake has a maximum depth of 2,000 feet and a diameter of almost six miles. No streams flow into the lake, and there are no visible outlets. The water is replenished . . . largely by snow falling directly into the lake during the winter months.

" 'Surrounding the lake are colorful cliffs, 500 to 2,000 feet high. . . . The cliffs tell a story of the building and destruction of a mighty volcano whose peak stood 5,000 to 7,000 feet above the present rim of the crater. The destruction of the peak of the ancient volcanic mountain, which may have surpassed in height any of the existing peaks of the Cascade range, resulted in the great crater now partially filled by the clear, fresh water of Crater Lake.' "

"Thank you, Stephen," said Mother. "Now, Marilyn, would you like to continue? There is an interesting Indian legend about the lake. Just tell us the story in brief."

" 'According to the legends of the Maklaks, ancestors of the Klamaths and the Modocs, the high mountain known to us as Mount Mazama was the home of Llao, a mythical Indian god,' " began Marilyn. " 'Llao's throne was deep in the lake's blue waters, where it was surrounded by the giant crawfish who were his warriors.

" 'Skell, who was the upper-world god of sunlight and fertile growth and all beautiful things, lived in the land east of the great marshes. He and Llao, through their terrible conflict over the love of a great chief's daughter, brought about the destruction of Mount Mazama.

" 'For seven days lightning darted like fire from the mountaintop, deep thunder shook the earth, winds howled throughout the forests, and dark smoke filled the sky.

" 'At last Llao's throne burst apart and, as fire rained over all the land, Llao killed Skell. The Coyote, the Fox, and the Golden Eagle brought back his heart, which had been thrown into the lake, and restored it to his body. Once again Skell lived and fought against Llao and his powers of darkness.

" 'Skell defeated Llao and threw his head into the lake, where it still remains as Wizard Island, and the cliff on which Llao was defeated is called Llao Rock. Although the curse of flaming fire never again came to Mount Mazama, at times great storms trouble the smooth surface of the lake.' "

Just as Marilyn finished the Indian legend, the car began to slacken speed.

"Oh, oh!" gasped Stephen and Marilyn, as their station wagon pulled up to the low-railed edge of a sheer drop. Quickly they got out and gazed in wondering awe upon the beautiful blue waters of Crater Lake.

For a long time the family remained in the same spot. At first the lake claimed their entire attention. Later on they watched with amusement the greedy chipmunks who scampered across nearby rocks and ran boldly near their feet.

"Just look at them!" laughed Stephen. "See this one! He's almost ready to eat bread right out of my hand."

"I'm about ready to eat it too," joked older brother Edwin Jess, as he and his wife Esther got out of their car and joined the family group.

"Don't you think we'd better go on up to Crater Lake Village before the middle of the afternoon?" he asked. "This lake is such a famous tourist attraction that people from all over the world come here. Many of them will have made camp already.

"We'd better find a good camping site before all the best locations are taken. Then we'll make up our beds snug and warm and build a fire in the camp stove. Darkness falls early in this high altitude, and evenings are downright cold even in summer months. You'll appreciate the warmth of a roaring fire."

By three o'clock the family group was thankful for Edwin Jess's advice. For when they reached the wooded area below Crater Lake Village, they found only one unoccupied camping site on the outer edge of the tourist zone. They hurriedly claimed the spot and began gathering firewood.

"We're not a moment too soon," stated Mother. "Now, while you men are making beds, the girls and I will start an early supper. Esther, would you peel and slice those boiled potatoes and several raw onions? Here's our big iron pancake griddle. It's just the thing for frying food to a turn.

"And will you please put the baked beans in the oven, Marilyn? They're still warm, but they'll taste much better if they're really hot. Then you can set the table. Isn't it nice to have a rustic table and log benches all ready and waiting for us?

"I brought our red-checked tablecloth and paper birthday napkins. You can put the big birthday cake for Dad and Stephen right in the center of the table. I used pink icing for Dad's name and green icing for Stephen's name. Doesn't it look pretty?"

"Pretty. And delicious!" exclaimed the girls, and Marilyn added, "Just to look at that rich, creamy frosting makes me as hungry as a bear!"

"Well, let's hope we don't have any hungry bears around here to share it with us," joked Mother. "I haven't any desire to meet one face to face out in these woods."

"Me either," puffed Stephen, setting down the bucket of cold spring water he had carried from a nearby faucet. "I'd like to see a bear when we're driving along, so I can tell the boys at school. But I don't want one for a camp mate."

"Oh, come on and wash your hands," urged Marilyn impatiently. "We haven't seen any wild animals larger than these chipmunks, and they are almost tame. I don't think it very likely we'll see any bears while we're right here with dozens of campers all around us."

"Well, I see some hungry people hurrying toward the table," Mother spoke quickly. "Let's put the food on the table. Then as soon as Dad says grace, we'll eat."

"When are we going to sing 'Happy Birthday'?" questioned Marilyn. "Right at first or when we cut the cake? I'd rather sing it now, because Dad and Stephen will see the cake before they sit down."

"All right, dear. Start us off as soon as everyone's through washing," nodded Mother.

"Happy birthday to you, happy birthday to you. Happy birthday, dear Dad and Stephen, happy birthday to you." The voices rang gaily in the clear mountain air.

"Well, well!" exclaimed Dad as he looked at the birthday decorations and the big iced cake. "This really is a surprise."

"Um-m-m!" exclaimed Stephen. He hungrily eyed the tempting dessert.

"I don't know when food ever tasted as good as this," sighed Edwin Jess a short while later. "This mountain air must sharpen one's appetite. I don't usually eat half as much as I did today."

"That's true," Dad nodded. "In fact, I could eat another small slice of that birthday cake. Mother, would you please——"

"Oh, look," Stephen gasped in an excited half whisper. "Look over there!"

"Where?" shrilled Marilyn. "I don't see anything."

"Right there by the garbage can. See? He's stuck his head down in the pail. Now he's falling over!"

BANG! CLATTER! CRASH!

"It's a bear," shrieked Marilyn. "It's a real live bear. I—I'm scared!"

"Sh-h!" cautioned Mother. "He's only looking for something to eat."

"Th-then let's g-give him s-s-some food so he'll go away," Marilyn shivered.

"No, don't do that," cautioned Edwin Jess. "All campers are warned not to feed the bears. And if you give him one morsel of food, he'll be back for more."

"Then we'll just sit quietly, and soon he'll surely go away," added Dad. "After all, there's nothing to fear. There are campers and picnickers on all sides of us and forest rangers not too far away."

"I wish they were a little closer," muttered Edwin Jess. "I don't like the looks of that rascal. He spells T-R-O-U-B-L-E in any language. It seems too bad we aren't permitted to carry firearms in the park. Once in a great while a revolver would come in mighty handy."

"I suppose it would," agreed Dad, "but not everyone knows how to use a gun wisely. For that reason no one can be permitted to shoot in a public park where a flying bullet might kill some person."

"Br-r-r!" whispered Marilyn. "I don't think that bear's going quietly away. He's—he's coming straight toward us!" She jumped up from the hard wooden bench, and her voice rose in a scream as the bear ambled in their direction.

"Don't run," warned Dad. "Be as quiet as you can. He may just be curious. But if you run, he might become angry and start after you. I think he'll go past us on the road. Anyway, we'll soon see."

"I'm not going to wait to find out," said Mother quickly. "Here, girls, let's start gathering up the food. That's right. Put the beans and salad in this box. Esther, can you reach the cake? Then put it in the smaller box. We can have it later in the evening after our hike. I'm sure we'll all be hungry again by that time."

"I'm afraid that bear's hungry right now," wailed Marilyn. "He—he's heading straight for us, and he's almost running."

"So am I," yelled Stephen. "Come on, folks. Grab the food, and let's get in our cars."

The scene became one of buzzing activity as each of the campers tried to save some portion of the food.

"Look out," shouted Edwin Jess. "He's going to jump up on the table. Be careful. Don't get near him. Stay back. I'm going to take some movies of this."

"I'll grab the cake box before he gets to it," volunteered Dad. "Stand back, everyone."

Stephen and Marilyn stopped and turned just in time to see Dad's hand reach out quickly toward the cake box. They stared in horror as they saw two brown furry paws flash toward the same box. They screamed as the bear's long, sharp fangs sank into the heavy cardboard container and the curving claws of one paw slashed across Dad's clutching hand.

"Let go, Dad. Let go!" yelled Stephen. He jumped up and down in excitement and fear as the four-legged thief ran triumphantly a short distance away and devoured their cake in two or three greedy gulps.

"Better run," cautioned Edwin Jess in a low voice. "He looks as though he'd return at any minute. And when he jumps back on the table and finds all the food put away, he'll likely attack us. We'd better get in our cars!"

"Yes, and lock the doors and roll up the windows," added Esther quickly.

"Hurry! Here he comes," yelled Stephen. He jumped into the station wagon and peered fearfully out the back window.

Gr-r-r! Gr-r-r-r-r!

They all stared toward the snarling creature on the dining table. They shuddered as they watched the ease with which his sharp claws ripped apart the several heavy paper boxes left behind in their hasty flight.

BANG! BANG! RATTLE! BANG! The noise made by nearby campers was deafening, but they saw that it did not frighten away the furry robber.

"Even those kettles and lids banging together don't scare him," stated Edwin Jess soberly. "There! He's going now, since he can find nothing else to eat. As soon as he's out of sight we'd better go to the ranger station and get your hand dressed, Dad. Scratches as long and deep as those can easily become infected without proper care."

"Whew!" Stephen exclaimed half-tearfully. "Doesn't your hand hurt just awful, Dad?"

"Well, it's far from being comfortable," Dad answered ruefully. "I just wish we had our forgotten first-aid kit that Marilyn left behind. Some of that alcohol would be useful right now before the blood congeals and hardens over these wounds."

"I—I'm sorry, Dad," Marilyn stammered. Her heart sank as she realized the serious result of her forgetfulness.

"Look. There's a ranger now!" shouted Stephen.

"And there's that bear, too. He's headed straight for those campers on the slope above us! See? Their baby's in his stroller out in the clearing!"

Stephen felt icy chills run up and down his back as he half fell out of the car and watched the ranger run toward the wild animal shambling toward the small child.

"My baby! My baby! Stop him," screamed the frantic mother.

"Stop him!" yelled the frightened father.

"Grab your baby," called the running ranger.

WHAM!

"There he goes!" Stephen yelled. He jumped up and down as the ranger's well-aimed rocks hit Mr. Bruin on the end of his nose and sent him scrambling up a tree.

"I'm packing up our bedrolls right now," declared Esther. "When that critter comes down from his high perch he may wander away through the hills and he may come right back here for more cake, bringing some of his pals. I don't intend to be on the reception committee if he does."

"Neither do I," agreed Mother. "I see that Edwin Jess has told the ranger about our attack. While Dad goes with him for some first-aid treatment, we'll break camp. We don't seem to be the only ones doing so either. Everyone else in our neighborhood is packing for departure."

"Well, I don't blame them," Stephen added. "I'm certainly not anxious to stay."

"Think of waking up at night and finding those beady eyes peering at you," shuddered Marilyn. "I'd just faint and fall on through the ground. I know I would."

It was some time before the excited group finished repacking. As the last bag was stowed away in Edwin Jess's car trunk, Dad drove up in the ranger's car. Stephen was the first to see the white bandage on his injured hand.

"Well, I guess we're ready to go," Dad said. "This ranger has requested that we stop at the main office three miles down the hill and file a complete report of the bear's attack. I heard him call on the telephone and say that we'd do so."

"What'd he say, Dad?" questioned wide-eyed Stephen. "Did he tell all about the bear clawing you?"

"Indeed he did," nodded Dad. "And he also said that this was a three-year-old who had previously caused trouble. The forest rangers have been trying to trap him for some time, but he's a very clever fellow who has always managed to escape."

"Will they shoot him when they catch him?" Stephen asked.

"No, they won't shoot him," Dad replied. "They'll put him in a small cage and take him some miles from here into the wilderness. There they will release him.

"However, if he comes back here, he will then be destroyed, as he has become dangerous."

"I'm sure of one thing," firmly stated Marilyn. "I'm not going to wander off in the direction of that particular wilderness. I've no desire to meet our uninvited dinner guest face to face. Once is enough for me."

"You're right," smiled Dad. "Now let's be on our way. First, we'll report to the park superintendent. We'll tell him we'll come back later on to finish our sight-seeing here.

"Then we'll go back to Diamond Lake. I don't think we'll find any wild creatures except chipmunks in camp there. In the morning we'll rent a motorboat and go for a ride on the lake."

Stephen looked anxiously at his father as he heard Mother ask, "Are you sure you're all right? Is your hand paining you a great deal? Perhaps we'd better go home and have the doctor look at those deep cuts."

He smiled as he heard Dad's reply. "No, I'll be all right. My hand's paining me some because the ranger probed quite deep when he cleansed the wound. But it will feel much better in a few hours. Let's go ahead with our birthday trip. Stephen and I aren't going to be cheated out of our fun. Are we, son?"

"No, Dad, we aren't," nodded Stephen. "We'll still get to camp out and hike and go on the lake. But I hope we don't have to serve dinner to any more wild animals. You and I certainly don't want to share any more of our birthday with hungry bears."

6

Cougar Rock

I WISH I could have a big dog like Max's St. Bernard. Of course, Blondie's all right, but she's really too little to be a first-class watchdog. She'd never be able to scare away burglars or pull me out of a river if I started to drown or—well, do anything brave like that. Would you, Blondie?" Stevie asked his tiny fox terrier, who sat looking up at him, her big brown eyes alight with love and devotion.

"That shows how ignorant you are about dogs, son," laughed Mrs. Smith, looking with amusement at the frowning boy. She knew that nothing in the world would ever persuade him to give up the white terrier who followed him about the house and yard all day and slept on a rug just outside his bedroom door at night. However, Raymond Jones' wealthy uncle had recently sent his young nephew a huge St. Bernard, and all the neighborhood boys were "green with envy." They did not stop to think what a nuisance the enormous animal would be when the family wanted to go out for a ride, or what great expense it would be to feed such a pet.

"Wait until I stir the potato soup that is cooking for supper, and I'll tell you a story that will make you appreciate the real courage of a small dog."

After a few moments Mrs. Smith returned to the living room, where Stevie and Blondie sat waiting for her.

"This happened many, many years ago, when my grandfather was a young man. He had been working about sixty miles from home, up in the McKenzie River region, which was then all dense timber, with only a rough wagon road leading across the mountains.

"He had finished his work in that particular section of the country and had spent several days walking down along the roadway that wound beside the beautiful, rushing McKenzie River, one of the scenic beauties of the West.

"His only companion and friend was Trixie, a wee black-and-white fox terrier who had been with him ever since grandfather had bought her as a tiny pup four years previous.

" 'Here is a lovely spot in which to eat our lunch and enjoy some of this dried venison, old girl,' he said, pausing to look at the grassy, sloping bank and moss-covered rocks in the pretty grove at the river's edge. 'There's a nice, quiet pool here, too, where we can drink. Come on.'

"He started down toward the place and then looked back. Trixie stood perfectly still, exactly where he had left her, only now her ears pointed straight up and the hair rose in a bristly ridge along her back.

" 'What in the world!' exclaimed Grandfather Brown. 'Trixie! Come along now.'

"A deep growl rumbled in Trixie's tiny throat. She did not even look at her master. Her keen eyes stared straight ahead down the road where, a short distance away, an enormous boulder rose skyward some twenty feet or more. It lay between the road and the river, and they would pass beneath its cool shade when they continued their journey.

" 'Stop that!' spoke grandfather sharply. Then he did something that he had never done before that time and which he always regretted afterward. He was hot and tired, and the dog's seeming disobedience angered him. Leaning over, he gave her a hard slap.

"Cringing, she followed him to their midday resting place, but though he offered her both food and water she refused them and lay motionless, nose sniffing the air, eyes fastened upon the rock.

" 'Can't think what ails that cur. She must have smelled out a rabbit or a chipmunk,' muttered grandfather to himself, as he finally rose and prepared to start out again. 'Hope she doesn't act like this the rest of the day, or I'll have to carry her in order to reach Trail's End Ranch by nightfall. And since I loaned my gun yesterday to friend Jones, I'm not anxious to be caught out after dark in the mountains. Too many wild animals, though they never bother humans in the daytime.'

" 'Come along,' he spoke disgustedly to his pet, who stiff-leggedly started to follow, breaking into gruff little growls every step or two.

"Grandfather strode impatiently ahead and did not

look back until Trixie yelped shrilly and then ran excitedly around and around him, pulling frantically at his
leggings.

" 'Stop it, you crazy dog,' he ordered, looking all
about them. He saw nothing to cause the slightest
alarm. The only moving object was his black-and-white
terrier, who ran noisily back and forth.

" 'I said to stop it,' he repeated, and, pushing her
aside, he hurried on. Within a few strides he was
opposite the tall, overhanging rock, whose upper half
jutted out over their path. Again Trixie pulled at his
clothing.

"There was a sudden terrific blow. It ripped slant-
wise upon his back, so that he staggered and almost fell
face downward. A sharp stinging sensation spread
across his shoulders, and blood began to drip down his
loosely ·rolled sleeves.

"A whirling cloud of dust from which arose fierce
deep growls, frantic barks, and at last a wild howl roused
him from his half-fainting condition, and he managed to
turn just in time to see a half-grown mountain lion, or
cougar, leaping into the woods, a limp little black-and-
white dog dangling from his clenched jaws.

"Grandfather Brown half walked and half fell down
to the river, where he lay for some time before he could
gather enough strength to wash his deep wounds. From
his resting place he could look up and see very plainly
the wide, almost hidden ledge upon which the mountain
beast had crouched, probably waiting for a young deer
to pass by. While it was unusual for one of his kind to
attack a man in the daytime, our family always thought

that it might have occurred because he was angered by Trixie's barking and because he was tempted by the smell of the dried deer meat slung in a large sack on the man's back.

"At any rate grandfather was a much sadder and wiser man as he crippled along, mourning the loss of his faithful watchdog and companion. As he told the story to friends at Trail's End Ranch that night, his eyes filled with tears as he stated how Trixie had vainly tried to warn him, and how he had punished her for being 'foolish.'

" 'There went the best friend a man ever had,' he said sorrowfully. 'Look for her? No, I didn't look for her. I was wounded and had no gun, and, anyway, how long do you think she'd have lasted with that big mountain lion? She'd make about one bite for him. No, I just figured that was the end of Trix. Poor little pet!' And grandfather, big strong man that he was, was not ashamed to take out his handkerchief and wipe his eyes."

In all this time Stevie had not once stirred. Now he let out his breath in a deep sigh, and tears filled *his* eyes as he cried, "Oh, Mother, how awful! That brave little dog. Why, he should have gone back to search for her. That wasn't one bit fair, after Trixie saved his life."

He caught up Blondie and held her tight in his arms, as though he half expected her to be snatched away by a pouncing beast.

Mother smiled. "But that isn't the end of my story. A few days later, after grandfather had somewhat recovered from his experience, he was walking in the woods near the ranch. Suddenly he heard faint, far-away barks. He stopped and listened. They grew louder and louder and closer and closer until finally, crashing through the underbrush came bounding——"

"The cougar!" exclaimed Stevie, wide-eyed.

"No," laughed mother. "It was Trixie. Faithful little Trixie had found her way back to her beloved master. Grandfather could scarcely believe his eyes as he saw her jumping up toward him, overjoyed at being with him once more. How she had escaped from her captor no one ever knew and, of course, Trixie could not tell. There were a number of scratches and one or two fairly deep bites on her body, but she soon recovered and was none the worse for her dangerous adventure.

"You may be sure that grandfather and Trixie were the talk of the valley for a while, and Trixie was so petted and praised by everyone that her owner vowed that she would be utterly spoiled.

"But the little terrier lived to a ripe old age, and as every wish of her dog heart was granted, I guess grandfather himself helped to spoil her if anyone did.

"And that is the end of the true story as to how Cougar Rock was given its name. And that is the end of the story of a brave little dog. Of course," added Mrs. Smith, slyly, "if Trixie had been a really large dog, such as a St. Bernard, for instance, she might have——"

"Pooh!" Stevie fiercely answered, hugging Blondie until she squealed, "I guess a fox terrier is just about the best watchdog anyone could have. Size doesn't mean very much, after all. Even if you're little you can be brave."

"I'm glad that you have learned a lesson from my story," smiled his mother. "Size doesn't count. And that is true of people as well as animals. It is the brave heart that helps one to win, whether the body surrounding that heart be large or small.

"But now, Stevie, you and Blondie must run up and get ready for the evening meal. We'll have another story tomorrow night."

7

Kerosene Kindling

C LANG, clang, clang, clang!
"Wake up, Dick. Hear
that fire bell? There's a big blaze somewhere." Jesse threw
back the bedcovers and sprang across the room, forgetful
for once of the damp winter chill in the big unheated
bedroom under the eaves. His long white underwear felt
warm and comfortable against his body as he pressed
his nose close to the windowpane and squinted down
the street.

"Say, it *is* a fire and a big one too. Hurry up, Slow-
poke. Come on over here. Look. You can see the sparks
shooting straight up into the sky. There goes the fire
engine. The horses are running as fast as they can. Look
at them!"

"Let's pull on our trousers and go see what's happening," Dick urged through his chattering teeth. "Br—
r—r. I'm so cold I can't find my clothes."

"They're probably right on the floor where you
stepped out of them at bedtime," tartly retorted Jesse.

He hastily grabbed his crumpled knee breeches from the brass footrail of the bed. "Better put on your sweater too, but we won't need any shirts. Come on. It must be the Jensen house. Maybe we can get there in time to help save some of their things. Lee and Harvey must be there by now. I don't hear them talking in their bedroom."

"Look at those flames," panted Dick as the boys neared the burning house. "We're too late to do anything. It's so hot that even the firemen can't get close enough with their hose, and if they could, that little stream of water wouldn't save the building."

"It's too bad," Jesse said soberly. He looked at the roof just in time to see it sag and fall inward with a crash that sent thousands of sparks spiraling into the night-blue sky. "I wonder if the Jensen family—oh, there they are."

"Where?" questioned Dick, anxious for the safety of his schoolmate, Chris.

"Right over there. See? Some of them are standing there in their night clothes. Let's go over and find out if they know what started the blaze." They raced quickly over to the stricken family.

"No, I don't really know what set the house on fire," Chris Jensen replied to Dick's question. "We'd gone to bed about nine o'clock—maybe it was nine-thirty— because Uncle Pete had come over, and we'd sat around the stove while he told us about his trip to San Francisco. He'd bought a new pipe up there, and he smoked it all evening to try to break it in. Mamma thinks maybe he knocked out some of the ashes and let them fall onto the rug. But we don't know for sure. Uncle Pete always did embarrass us with his smoking. Father had often tried to get him to give up the filthy habit.

"All I do know is that we were sound asleep when papa yelled, 'Fire, fire! Run for your lives!' I just grabbed what I could and jumped down the stairs three at a time. I picked up my knee breeches all right, but I got only one stocking and one shoe. I'll sure look funny at school tomorrow wearing only a pair of pants and one stocking and one shoe."

"Never mind, Chris!" The three boys turned as Dad Hayden's comforting voice sounded in their ears. "You come on over to our house for the rest of the night. We'll see that you have something to wear to school in the morning. The neighbors will help find clothes for all your family, and give each of you a place to stay until your father and mother can get located again.

"We managed to save most of the heavy furniture, because we grabbed that first. But many smaller articles had to be left behind. The fire got so hot that we could make only two or three trips back and forth. But we saved enough articles so that your parents can set up housekeeping again.

"Now you boys had better go on home and try to get some sleep. Mother and Thelma will be worried half to death, wondering what's going on. I didn't want them to come out in the night air. You can tell them that everyone's safe and that I'll be home later. I'm going to stay awhile. Some of us will get the furniture under cover in that old shed on the back of your lot, Chris. It shouldn't be left out in the night air or the morning sunlight.

"Hurry along now. There'll be school tomorrow, the same as usual. And I know three boys who'll be mighty big sleepyheads at six o'clock in the morning."

After hurrying home through the dark night the three boys, all talking at once, tried to explain to Mother Hayden all that had happened. Jesse saw that she listened carefully and, in the mysterious fashion of mothers, seemed to understand exactly what each one was saying.

"Oh, how dreadful," she exclaimed when they had finished their stories. "Chris, I'm so sorry that you've lost your home. But I'm thankful that none of you were burned. Kind friends can help replace the articles that you have lost, but none of us could bring back the life of a loved one. Fire can be a great blessing to mankind. But when it is carelessly used it can be a cruel and devouring enemy.

"But now you must all go to bed. I knew you'd be tired and cold with all the excitement, so I built up the fire in the cookstove and heated some milk. Each of you boys must drink a mugful of hot milk. Then you'll be able to sleep well."

Over the brown mug of steaming milk Jesse smiled gratefully at his gentle little mother. He thought again how understanding she was and how she always managed to do the right thing at the right time.

"Not a bit like me," he muttered to himself as he led the way up the narrow winding stairs into the chilly bedchamber. "I'm always doing the right thing at the wrong time or the wrong thing at the right time—or—well——"

"What on earth are you mumbling about?" Dick questioned curiously, following closely on his brother's heels. "What's the matter with you?"

"Oh, nothing," Jesse answered sharply, embarrassed at being caught holding conversation with himself. "Come on, Chris. You can sleep with us. Last one in bed's a monkey and has to sleep in the middle."

Three pairs of knee breeches slid to the gray rug. Two pairs of shoes and one solitary shoe clattered against the floor boards. Three forms clad in underwear hurled themselves upon the big bed, wrestled briefly for the best sleeping places, and then sank gratefully against the warmth of the gray woolen blankets.

"I thought I'd stay awake all night, but I'm so sleepy I can't hold my eyes open. It must have been that hot milk," whispered Chris, worn out with the evening's excitement. "Good night, boys. See you in the morning."

"Night," chorused Jesse and Dick while Dick added, "Me too. I'll be asleep in two shakes of a lamb's tail."

But long after the two younger boys lay snoring Jesse stared wide-eyed into the blackness. He saw again the red, licking flames as they curled and writhed around the white pillars of the Jensen porch and then shot through the open doorways of the doomed home. Even after he fell asleep he kept dreaming of the clanging fire engine with its two heavy draft horses. He kept hearing the frightening clang, clang, clang of the fire bell as it shattered the calm stillness of the night.

The next day's recess periods at school were entirely given over to telling and retelling the story of the disastrous fire. On every side Jesse heard snatches of excited conversation as little groups of wide-eyed school children told each new bit of information that came their way.

"They were sound asleep in their beds when the fire started."

"Chris said it must have been caused by sparks from his uncle's pipe, because his father doesn't smoke."

"They didn't save any clothes at all except the ones they grabbed up as they ran out of the house."

"My folks gave them something to wear, so they'd be warm and not have to buy new clothes. My father said it'd cost lots of money to have to buy new clothing for all of them."

Even during school hours Jesse heard whispered bits of the information until it seemed to him that the teacher might just as well dismiss classes for the rest of the day And then after school he was joined by a group of older boys who walked slowly away from the schoolhouse.

"Guess that really was *some* fire last night, wasn't it, Hayden?" asked Lem, the ringleader of this older gang. "Did you see the whole thing? Of course, none of us knew anything about it until we came to school. We all live too far away to get in on the fun."

"Y—Yes, I saw the fire," stammered Jesse. "But I wouldn't call it fun." He swallowed hard in his excitement at being noticed by this superior group of teen-age youth who until now had openly despised all the younger boys at school. His cheeks flushed as he told the story of the night's events, and his feet followed unheedingly in the direction set by Lem as the older boy asked question after question.

"Say, I'm going the wrong way," blurted Jesse as he

roused from his hero-worshiping trance. "I—I guess I got so interested in talking to you that I forgot I should have headed down Elwood Street. Dick and Chris'll be wondering where I am. I—I've got to go now, so good-by."

"Here, here. Not so fast, Hayden," he heard Lem say flatteringly. "Your brother Dick and Chris are too young to join our gang, but we thought you'd make a pretty good member. You've got enough pep to keep up with us, and you're broad-minded enough to join in with us on our fun. Some of these sissies at school are such tattletales we can't have them around. But we've decided you'd be all right.

"How about it? Want to belong to the Daredevil Club? This is your one and only chance, so speak up, quick."

Join the Daredevil Club. So this was actually the much-talked-about Daredevil Club! Jesse breathed quickly and wondered whether they could hear the pounding of his rapidly beating heart. "Why," he thought excitedly, "not even Lee or Harvey has been invited to join them, and yet they've asked me to be a member. What should I say?"

"I—why—well, you see—I——" he stammered out before Lem's impatient voice cut across his reply with the sharpness of a keen knife.

"Don't stutter so, Hayden," he sneered. "You sound like that broken gramophone record at school." Jesse felt his new-found importance shrivel with embarrassment at the mocking scorn in the ringleader's changing voice.

"Do you want to be a Daredevil? Or do you want to be a dare nothing! Answer up. We haven't got all day to carry out our plans. If you don't join, we'll ask somebody else who'll jump at the chance to be a member."

Jesse felt as though he couldn't bear to say No, and be the target of the unkind laughter that he knew would roll forth from the throats of the grinning youths who stood around him. Wild thoughts and scrambled bits of past conversations heard at home and at school rushed through his perplexed mind and stifled the Yes that his boyish heart yearned to say.

"That group of boys will come to no good end. Mark my words, they're heading straight for trouble. Policeman Murphy told me he caught them down at the warehouse one night. They hadn't broken in and done any damage, but he's sure that they were planning to do so."

"Did you hear about the Daredevil Club? The principal said he'd expel them if he found out who they were and caught any of them in trouble. They won't tell who belongs, you know. It's against school rules to belong to any kind of secret club."

Jesse was never quite sure what his exact answer would have been, because at that moment Lem caught him by the arm and dragged him along at his side. "Look down the street," he said breathlessly. "There's the kerosene wagon stopping by the Corner Grocery. Hurry up. We're going to watch the driver fill the big kerosene cans at the back of the store."

"Wh—what for?" gulped Jesse breathlessly. He tried hard to pull back from the long-legged pace set by the taller youth. "I—I can't—run—so fast."

"Aw, come along, baby," sneered Lem as Jesse felt his tightening grasp. "We'll show you some real fun pretty soon."

"F—fun?" panted Jesse. He was thankful that they had reached their destination and had come to an abrupt halt in the dirt street that bordered the side of the wooden structure known as the Corner Grocery. "I don't see that it's any fun to stand here and look at the store. I come here lots of times on errands for mamma, and I've never seen anything funny around here."

"Listen, fellows. Our little boy comes here on errands for his mamma," Jesse heard Lem say in a high whining voice. "Isn't he a good little mamma's boy? Don't you think he's just the one who can do a nice little errand for us?"

"I—I don't think I want to join your club, after all," Jesse stammered. "P—please let go my arm, Lem. I—I've got to go home and cut kindling wood for the kitchen stove. That's one of my chores."

As he heard the group's coarse laughter, Jesse tried to shrink away from his captor. With all his heart he wished that he had not stopped to talk with Lem and his companion club members, much less accompany them to this spot, for he sensed that whatever they meant to do was not right. Again he tried to pull away, but again he felt Lem's big hand hold tight to his sleeve.

"Just a minute, cherub, and then you can run home," Lem laughed. "But now watch, and you'll see what I've been talking about. We're going to show you how to cut some real kindling that'll burn in a hurry—kerosene kindling. Just be mighty sure you don't tell anyone about it either, or you'll get what's coming to tattletales. I'll see to that."

Held fast in Lem's relentless grip, Jesse stared in puzzlement. He glanced quickly from the grinning faces of the Daredevil Club members to that of the whistling driver who had just finished filling the big kerosene barrels nestled against the back of the store. He watched as the man lifted the still-dripping emptied buckets into the delivery wagon, climbed into the high wagon seat, and drove away.

He watched wonderingly as Lem pointed to the kerosene trail that led straight to the store's brimming barrels. He stared as he saw him nod his head quickly. Puzzled, he sniffed the acrid sulphur smell of the burning match that the tallest club member scratched on his shoe and flung gleaming into the nearest little kerosene puddle. And then, horrified and unable to move, Jesse saw the little match flame burst full blown into a crimson, fiery flower. He watched, horrified and unbelieving, as it spread and changed shape until it became a fiery rope that stretched from his feet to the wooden store's back porch.

"Run, boys, run," yelled Lem.

Dimly Jesse heard their retreating footsteps. Dimly he realized that he stood alone. But still he could neither move nor free himself from the dreadful waking nightmare that gripped him. And then he heard the roar of the flaming kerosene barrels. He saw the fiery shower that sprayed up along the board walls and across the back yard and the dirt road. The heat of the searing fire reached him before he began to run toward safety.

His feet pounded so hard on the board sidewalk that he scarcely heard the frightened voices of the store's occupants as they ran outside, screaming, "Fire, fire!"

Jesse felt his breath whistle in his throat. He felt a keen knifelike pain stab again and again in his aching side. He felt his high-topped shoes growing heavier and heavier. But he dared not stop or look back until he reached the picket fence around his home. Only then did he cast a fearful glance over his shoulder, half expecting to see both the store owner and the leaping flames pursuing him down the road.

He ran around the house, through the back door, and up the winding stairway, thankful that neither mother nor his little sister Thelma were in the kitchen to question him. Without pausing he flung himself on the floor and rolled under the bed, where he lay for what seemed to him hours and hours. As he heard footsteps and voices he pressed his head against the cold floor. His eyes smarted as he listened to his mother's voice inquiring, "But where *is* Jesse? Suppertime's already past. He should have been home by now."

Then he thought that he must have dozed, for he knew it was much later when he heard the soft rustle of his mother's long skirts. His lips trembled as she knelt beside the bed and spoke softly to him.

"Jesse, Jesse, are you there, my boy? Come on out. It's mother. I have something for you."

"O, Mother," Jesse groaned, now fully awake and positive that a policeman would soon come to drag him away to jail. "I—I didn't do anything. Honest I didn't. But dad'll never believe me."

Slowly, achingly, he pulled himself out from under the bed and looked up into his mother's sympathetic face. When he saw the lamplight shining on her smooth brown hair and on her gentle, understanding smile, he felt the hot tears prick against his eyelids.

"But I didn't do anything wrong, Mother," he choked. "At first I thought it'd be fun to be a member of the Daredevil Club. But after Lem made me go with him and wouldn't let loose of my arm, I knew I didn't want to stay with them. Then when he said I'd be the one who'd get the blame for throwing that lighted match into the kerosene I—I hated him, Mother. He's a bad boy. And I don't want to have anything to do with him or any of the others in his club."

"No, Jesse, you mustn't associate with boys like that," he heard his mother reply. "But you must not hate them either, though it is all right to hate their wrong-doing.

"Those boys have been caught, and they will have to work many long hours to repay the owner for the damage done to his store. Fortunately only the back part of the building was burned, for enough men were in the neighborhood to put out the flames before they had eaten their way into the main room. Mr. Clark was much more fortunate than the Jensen family."

"But—but, Mother," Jesse stammered, "how did anyone know who started the fire? Those boys ran away the minute they threw that match down in the kerosene. I was the only one who didn't run. And I'll be the only one Mr. Clark will blame!"

"No, son, you needn't worry," his mother continued.

"You see, since you boys hadn't come home from school, Thelma had gone to the store for me. She and Mr. Jensen happened to be walking together along the back street. They saw the whole thing. You can be sure Mr. Jensen lost no time telling the authorities about it too. He knew who was to blame. And you can also be sure that Thelma lost no time in running home and telling us exactly what had happened.

"But now, come on over to the washstand. I've brought up a pitcher of warm water so that you can wash your face and hands. Here's a clean towel too. There. You look better, I must say.

"Now take off your clothes and put on your flannel nightgown. I declare, I do believe you boys would always sleep in your underwear if you had the chance. I'll kneel down with you while you say your prayers. And then I want you to drink this good hot milk. There's nothing like a hot drink to put one to sleep. I didn't want my boy up here all alone, hungry and fearful. So I just heated this and brought it up to you."

"But how did you know where I was?" Jesse inquired. He sat bolt upright in his bed and stared round-eyed over the steaming big mug that he held in both hands. "I came in as quiet as I could so no one would know where I was. Did you see me, Mamma?"

Jesse never forgot his mother's reply as she said, "No, Jesse, I didn't see you—that is, not with my eyes. But my heart told me where you'd be—my poor frightened boy.

"Always remember, son, no matter what happens and no matter what you have done, dad and mother love you. We'll stand by you and help you in any way we can. So never be afraid to come to us.

"I'm glad you didn't really want to be a Daredevil. I'm glad that you were not one of the guilty boys today. But, even if you had been, we'd have loved you and tried to help you to be a good boy.

"And now, Jesse, good night. And may God bless and keep you always."

Long after his mother had left the darkened room Jesse lay awake, listening contentedly to the voices of the family downstairs. He heard his father's deep tones, his mother's soft, low replies. the laughing voices of his brothers, and little Thelma's childish tones. He listened as they talked excitedly about their forthcoming plans for moving to their new home in Oregon.

Then, just before he drifted into slumber, he seemed again to hear his mother saying, "Always remember, son, no matter what happens, dad and mother love you."

Her voice seemed to mingle with the faraway clang of the fire bell, rising and falling in time to its clanging rhythm. But Jesse only pulled the covers up around his ears and snuggled closer into his warm nest.

"Fires and more fires and kerosene fires. What a day!" he thought drowsily. "I'm glad it's over. But I'm more glad I've got a dad and mother who understand. For their sake I'm never going to be tempted into being a Daredevil. If it means getting into trouble, I'd rather be a dare nothing. I'd rather——"

But Jesse was sound asleep.

8

Riding on a Thunderbolt

JESSE AND Dick walked proudly around and around their new red racing bug. Their eyes shone as they looked at its sturdy plank body and roller-bearing wheels.

"That old broom handle of dad's was just the thing for the steering rod," mumbled Dick. "I'm glad he hasn't missed it yet." He leaned over the "engine's" hood to run his dirty hands over the twisted ropes which were wrapped tightly around the broomstick and fastened to the front axles.

"This is the best racer we've ever made," stated twelve-year-old Jesse. "We've been building these bugs for three years. And we've held the Fairmount Boulevard championship for the last year. Willie and Ralph took the prize the first time. But they've not beaten us since then."

"They're not going to beat us this time, either!" stoutly agreed ten-year-old Dick. He raised a grease-stained face to look at his brother. "I know it'll coast like a charm. We've certainly worked hard to get our *Thun-*

105

derbolt finished in time for the big Hill race this week end. Say, Jesse, do you think the paint's dry enough? If it is, let's pull our bug over to the boulevard and try it out."

"It's dry," nodded Jesse. "Come on. I'm anxious to see if that long stick nailed on the side will work all right. If it doesn't, we'll have to fix another kind of brake. It's too dangerous to make that mile-long run without any way of stopping."

The new racing car made its trial race down the steep, winding boulevard that overlooked Eugene, and at the end of the ride the boys stared breathlessly at each other.

"Whew!" exclaimed Dick. "I never expect to travel any faster than I did that time. I'll bet we were going fifty miles an hour."

Jesse nodded as he squinted at the setting sun. "It's a dandy, all right. I want to test that brake some more, though. It doesn't work the way it should. But right now we'd better head back up the homeward trail. Dad'll soon be coming up the hill. I just remembered that he told us to be sure to build the fire and cook some potatoes and carrots."

"Aw, let's take one more coast," begged Richard. "Harvey ought to be home by now. Let him do the work."

Jesse shook his head. "Harvey won't be there until late. We'd better hurry!"

He started up the road with his pouting younger brother helping to push their *Thunderbolt* on the homeward journey.

Although the two boys hurried, the sun had set and dusk had fallen by the time they reached their Chula

Vista Park home. The faint gleam of a kerosene lamp in the kitchen told them that their hard-working father was there. Ever since their mother's death, a year before, he had been both father and mother to them. He not only provided a good living but also did the cooking and canning, the housework and cleaning. Usually he was most patient, but tonight he was tired. And he was cross because the two younger boys had again forgotten their home duties.

"I thought that I told you boys to build a fire and start supper," he said. He looked at them over his spectacles.

"Yes—yes, Father, you did," stammered Jesse. "We —we didn't know it was so late, or we'd have come home sooner. We'll hurry up and fix the potatoes now."

"The potatoes and other vegetables are almost done," their father answered shortly. "I have to go to a meeting tonight. For that reason I was anxious to have you start the meal. Where have you been? Out coasting on Fairmount Boulevard?"

The two boys nodded their close-cropped heads. Their father tightened his lips. He looked at them for a moment before he spoke.

"You are not to coast on that hill for one week," he declared firmly. "Perhaps by that time you can remember to do what you are asked."

"But, Father——" began two wailing voices. "The racing contest is this week end, and——"

"Not another word," their father interrupted. "You've been getting more and more careless about minding me. This may teach you a lesson."

Jesse and Dick looked at each other with tear-blurred eyes. Their healthy appetites seemed to vanish. They barely nibbled at the good dinner which their father set before them. But in bed that night they whispered to each other for a long time before they finally fell asleep.

The day of the race dawned bright and clear. Jesse and Dick rose early. As soon as breakfast was over and the dishes were washed they began working in the family orchard. For an hour or two after their father had gone they kept on. At last Dick threw down his hoe.

"I'm sick and tired digging away in this hard ground," he snapped. "I think we've done enough work the last four days to make up for a whole month's time."

He looked down at his bare feet and scuffed them in the dirt before he again spoke. "Let's get out our new racer and go on over to the Hill. I saw Willie and Ralph go past Reed's house quite a while ago. They were pulling their old racing bug. I just know ours will be the best one there. We're sure to have the fastest racer on the hill. I think it's mean of dad to tell us we couldn't go."

"We—e—ll, he didn't exactly say we couldn't go," hesitated Jesse. "He just said we couldn't coast for a week. But that was four days ago. We've really worked awfully hard since then. Maybe he's forgotten all about it by now. I wonder—— All right, let's get *Thunderbolt* and go to the boulevard."

Fifteen racing bugs were lined up by the time Jesse and Dick reached the top of the Hill, and a number of onlookers stood along the winding road.

"Hello, there," called Willie and Ralph. "We thought you weren't coming!"

Jesse and Dick grinned as they waved to their neighbors, the Paasche boys.

"Oh, we thought we'd surprise you!" Jesse answered. "We didn't want anyone to see our new racing bug until just time for the race to begin."

"That isn't what my father said last night," excitedly added Ralph. "He said that your father told him that you boys couldn't coast on the boulevard for one week. He'll be mighty angry if he finds out that you've disobeyed him."

"Pooh! How's he going to find out unless you're a tattletale!" interrupted Dick. "We're not going to say anything about it unless we win the race."

"Yes, if we win the race maybe he'll be so proud of us that he won't punish us for coming!" said Jesse. "But look! here's Mr. Thompson now. He's ready to start the races."

Each racing car owner drew a number from a hat. Jesse was the last one to turn over the little slip of paper and learn his place in the contest. He saw that he had drawn number sixteen. He and Dick were in the last group of four racers to speed down the winding driveway.

"One!" yelled Willie. "We got number one. We'll give you a run that'll make your hair stand on end. Just see if we don't."

Car by car the first four homemade racing bugs lined up across the road. At a given signal they started off. Jesse and Dick craned their necks to watch them go faster and faster down the pavement strip that curved along the upper end of Fairmount Hill.

"They're really traveling!" cried Dick. Jesse nodded his head.

The winner of this group, Paasches' racer *Lightning*, was selected amid cheers from the crowd. The second of the group of four raced down side by side, and their winner was selected by the judges. The third group did the same. Then at last it was time for the fourth group. The four racers lined up evenly, with Jesse and Dick as number sixteen. Dick sat at the wheel of their car.

"Get ready—get set—go!" shouted the signalman.

Jesse pushed forward with all his might against the back of their *Thunderbolt* and then sprang onto the rear framework. He clung tightly to the seat as they swerved around the first corner. They went so fast that they seemed to reach the end of the boulevard almost before they had time to draw a long breath. Without a doubt Jesse and Dick had easily won first place in their group.

This time the race was between the winner of each group. Again four racers lined up awaiting the downward flash of the signalman's arm. This time Jesse and Dick saw the Paasche boys grinning at them from the outer curb position.

"Better watch out!" yelled Willie. "We're going to win!"

"Ready! Go!" yelled Mr. Thompson.

Again they whizzed down, neck and neck with Willie and Ralph. The third and fourth racers bumped into each other at the turn into Feldman's yard and rolled over against the rosebushes. They were out of the running. The only two cars left to finish the contest were the Paasches' *Lightning* and Jesse and Dick's *Thunderbolt*.

The two bugs finished hood to hood, which made neces-sary another race between them.

The third and last time Jesse and Dick pushed their shiny red car into position on the starting line.

"Willie and Ralph have a good racer," whispered Jesse into his brother Dick's ear. "Stay close to the curb all the way down. Don't take a chance on getting out in the middle of the road near them. They'll go like greased lightning and our brakes are no good at all. I tried it at the foot of the hill on that last run. It didn't slow us up a bit."

"Go!" yelled the signalman. Jesse outdid himself with an extra-strong shove. He jumped on the back of the car just in time to catch a glimpse of Paasches' *Lightning* a half length behind them.

Faster and faster spun the metal-rimmed wheels. Faster and faster and faster. With a swing they rounded the first curve.

"Yippee!" Jesse dared a quick glance backward.

"Faster!" he yelled into Dick's ear. "We're pulling away. Duck your head. Lean forward more."

The two boys crouched lower. Their young bodies strained forward in their eagerness to gain greater speed for their *Thunderbolt*.

"Pull 'er round!" groaned Jesse, as they neared the most dangerous curve of all. "Pull in close to the curb!" Dick's knuckles whitened on the steering wheel. His red lips tightened.

Scre—eech! Their *Thunderbolt* swayed wildly, righted itself, and flashed onward with Paasches' *Light-ning* now a full length behind.

"One more curve and we've won!" yelled Jesse into his brother's ear. "Just one more curve!"

"I can't pull in!" shouted Dick. "We're going too fast. I can't."

He half straightened with a gasp. "You're too far out in the road. Swing back, Dick! Pull in close! Quick."

Too late! Their *Thunderbolt* rounded the last turn in a wide swing. Squarely in front of them loomed a high-axled Model-T Ford. For a second Jesse looked into the staring eyes of the white-faced man at the wheel. There was a sickening crash. Then all was blackness!

Jesse struggled half awake, to find himself lying in a crumpled heap in the middle of the pavement. He heard excited voices.

"He's coming around all right. Bad cut on his upper lip, though. Seems to be cut clear through and bleeding pretty bad. We'd better get him to a doctor as fast as we can."

"You're right," spoke a second voice. "But do you think we ought to move the younger boy? He looks mighty white. I'm afraid he has some broken bones."

Jesse tried to open his heavy eyelids. He tried to ask about his brother and Willie and Ralph. But no words came. Great waves of pain rose higher and higher. At last he fell into a black depth and heard no further sounds.

When Jesse again awoke he and Dick lay in their own beds in their own room. Their serious-faced father sat on a chair near them, and their married sister Lottie moved quietly about the room.

"What—where—where are we?" gasped Jesse. He

felt gingerly of the bandage that covered his face. "Ouch! it hurts."

"I suspect it does, son," nodded his father. "And I'm afraid that it will hurt even more before it becomes any better. The doctor had to take a few stitches in that gash underneath your nose. It was a nasty wound."

"And—and Dick. Is he—is——?"

"He's going to be all right, Jesse. But he, too, will have a long, hard time getting well. The doctor found that three ribs were torn loose from his back. Dick also has many cuts and bruises. He will have to be quiet for some time. Both of you were knocked unconscious."

"And Willie and Ralph?" weakly questioned Jesse.

"They swung their racer over to the curb and managed to pass the Ford safely. You boys hit the car dead center. Your racer went under the car while you hit and broke the headlight with your head. Then you and Dick fell off under the Ford, but the wheels did not run over you. In spite of your injuries you were very fortunate to have escaped death."

"If it's any comfort to you," added Lottie, "I'll say that you and Dick almost won the race. The Paasche boys' racer jumped over the curb, so no one reached the finish line. Maybe that'll cheer you somewhat, for your father says that this is the end of your racing days on Fairmount Boulevard."

"Well, anyway," groaned Jesse, "I don't think I ever want to race again. I'm sure that it's dangerous business for us to try *riding on a Thunderbolt*."

9

Mystery of Malheur Cave

EDWIN BOUNCED joyfully up and down on the back car seat as his father turned off the main highway onto the little-used side road leading to Malheur Cave. Burning heat waves shimmered on the surface of the lonely sagebrush-covered desert plateau, where the only moving things in sight were the car, whirling clouds of dust, and a bounding, startled jack rabbit.

"What fun! Only to think that last month we were in Sea Lion Caves on the Pacific Ocean, and now we get to see another cave away over here in eastern Oregon," spoke Edwin, leaning forward.

"That's right, son," Mr. Geary nodded, smiling, but never ceasing to drive carefully. "I believe that you'll find this as interesting and unusual in its way as the coastal cavern. And although there are no roaring sea lions to greet you, you may be fortunate enough to find a few silent messengers at the entrance."

"Messengers? At the entrance?" questioned the wide-eyed boy. "Why Dad, you said that this spot was absolutely deserted. Do people live here? I don't see how they could." His puzzled glance roved over the houseless miles of high desert.

Mr. Geary chuckled quietly while Mrs. Geary smiled. "Your father is only trying to arouse your interest, Edwin, but he doesn't need to worry about your enthusiasm, I'm sure. The silent messengers are the pointed arrowheads that have lain in the cave for a number of years. However, I doubt that many are now left, for the entrance has been widened so that the few sightseers who come to this out-of-the-way spot find it easy to enter. But we'll soon be there to find out for ourselves."

"Soon be there?" Edwin exclaimed. "Why, look how far away the mountains are. And we're still right out here on flat ground. I'll bet we are miles and miles from a hole in the mountain."

Just before driving over the little incline a few yards ahead, Mr. Geary turned the car off the road and came to a stop in the sagebrush.

"There you are, son," he said, pointing ahead toward a little gully. There is the entrance to mysterious Malheur Cave."

"Why, you can hardly see it. It's hidden from the roadway," exclaimed Edwin. He plunged out of the car and raced to the low-roofed and jagged entrance, while Mr. and Mrs. Geary gathered up the articles needed for their trip, and Mrs. Geary carried over Edwin's wool sweater and handed it to him.

"I don't need this, Mother," he protested. "I'll bet it's 100 degrees in the shade right now."

"Take it along, just the same," insisted Mrs. Geary. "I have been here before, and I can promise you that before long you'll be glad to have a warm wrap. The temperature in here is never very high."

The Gearys stood side by side and looked ahead for several hundred feet into a huge cavern, the dome of which rose quickly from the low entrance to about thirty feet in height. As they started forward on the hard-packed dirt floor they found that it slanted steadily downward for some distance. They passed a great pile of rocks in the middle of the trail and then turned to the right, entering a large natural chamber 60 feet wide. Here they stopped, for from this point onward the light from the cave mouth could not be seen. All was in darkness.

"Br-r!" shivered Edwin. "They had electric lights in Sea Lion Caves, and it wasn't as black as this. Isn't there any electricity here?"

"No, dear," his mother replied. "This natural wonder is many miles from any town, and it has never been made over for tourists. We shall have to accept it as it is, just as did the Indians who once hid in here. However, instead of flaring torches we have our flashlights and gasoline lantern to light the way. There! Now we can see quite well, but walk carefully. The trail becomes rougher and covered with boulders, and it is also quite slippery."

"How can plain old dirt be slippery?" asked the human question box, "when we're away out here in the desert with no water near us."

"That's where you are mistaken," spoke up Mr.

Geary. "These walls ooze moisture, which drips down to form large mud puddles. Further on after about a fifteen-minute walk, you'll see plenty of water. Just wait and see."

Edwin scrambled along as best he could, excited by his father's last remark. What did he mean?

Suddenly their lights flashed upon perfectly smooth and crystal-like water. "Here we are, almost at journey's end," said Mr. Geary. "We have walked a quarter of a mile on land, and here is Paiute Lake, which affords the only quarter-mile underground boat ride in the entire West."

"Is this boat safe enough for rowing?" questioned Mother Geary doubtfully.

After a careful inspection they climbed in and pushed off from shore. Edwin hung over the boat's edge, fingers trailing in the mirrorlike water.

"I can see something shining in the bottom," he cried. "It looks like a gold chain. Stop a minute, and I'll reach down." Mrs. Geary gasped; his father jerked him back. "Sit down, Edwin, and don't do that again."

Edwin's lip trembled. "But—but why, Daddy? I didn't mean any harm. It's so shallow that I just thought I'd reach down to the bottom and——"

"Son, this underground lake is over twenty feet deep. No one knows its source or its outlet and I am not anxious to have you fall in. Do you notice how the rock roof curves downward at this very spot? We have reached the end of our journey."

They had rowed back to shore and had just begun the return trip by land when Edwin spoke.

"Mother, you mentioned Indians hiding in the cave. Did they really live here for a while?"

"Indeed, they did," she responded. "Malheur Cave was an Indian stronghold in early days. If we travel along slowly, I'll tell you one of the most interesting of the many legends which have been woven about it. It was told to me by Mr. Julian Byrd, editor of the Burns *Times-Herald*. It dates back far beyond the time of aged Chief Louie of the Paiutes who died when I was only a little girl. Can you hear me as we walk along?"

"Oh, yes, I can," the youngster answered. "Go ahead, Mother, please. I'd love to hear about it."

And so Mrs. Geary, in the inky blackness in which their little lights only faintly gleamed, told the story of why Malheur Cave was found barricaded by the white men.

"A long, long time ago—many, many moons ago —before any white man came to this country, Malheur Lake was full of water. This water flowed out through the river channel past Malheur Cave.

"In these early days a large party of Paiute Indians, including men, women, and children, traveled this route and camped on the lake border. Here the children and women worked hard, gathering roots, herbs, and seeds to dry in preparation for the freezing winter weather.

"After a time a number of Bannock Indians from Idaho came along and camped with them. For a while all was peace and contentment. Then, alas, an epidemic swept like wildfire through the two tribes, and old and young among the Paiutes and Bannocks began dying off like flies. The medicine men worked furiously, dancing and chanting, but to no avail. The air was filled with groans and weeping and wailing.

"The Paiute medicine men became frightened. Fearing that their people would blame them for the many deaths, they decided to place the blame upon the Bannock Indians.

" 'The Bannocks! The Bannocks!' they screamed and shouted. 'They brought this awful death upon us. They are to blame. Let us kill them. Then we shall once more be well and strong.'

"At once the remaining Paiutes fell upon their neighbors with such fury that, with the exception of a small handful, all were slain. These escaped under cover of darkness and fled to Idaho, where they told their tribesmen of the Paiutes' treachery.

"A large war party of Idaho Bannocks immediately set forth to avenge their dead companions. While yet a few days' journey from the lake they rested one evening about their campfire, making mouth-filling boasts of their bravery and of the awful fate which awaited the Paiute Indians at their hands.

"However, unseen by them, Coyote had slipped into their midst and, ears pricked forward, was listening closely to their talk, for he was a friend of the Paiutes.

"Coyote hurried ahead to warn his friends. 'Quick,' he called. 'Gather food and blankets and firewood, and hurry to Malheur Cave. There, with its stream of

living water, you can hold out forever against the Bannocks, who are on the warpath. Hurry, my friends. Run for your lives.'

"The Paiutes hastened to the underground hiding-place. A rock barricade covered the cave entrance and behind it they settled down, unafraid.

"When the Bannocks rushed fiercely upon them, sending hundreds of sharp-tipped arrows flying harmlessly into the narrow entrance, the Paiutes only laughed, for they were safe from all danger.

"After many weeks the Bannocks had to admit their defeat and return to Idaho, and faithful Coyote hurried to tell his Paiute brothers that all was well and that they could at last come safely forth into the daylight.

"The happy Paiutes removed only enough rocks to make an exit for a hasty departure. That is why the white men found the entrance to Malheur Cave almost hidden with rocks and why hundreds of arrows were discovered in the cave and at its entrance.

"And that is why the Paiutes in the days of long, long ago honored Coyote and would not harm him. They believed him to be the most cunning and the most wise of all animals. And it was he, they believed, who received the soul of the Indian and lived on in bliss in a happy hunting ground where all was happiness and contentment."

The Gearys rounded the turn and blinked in the light from the entrance.

"Why, I feel as though I'd been on a long journey," Edwin said as they turned off their lights and walked toward the entrance. "That was certainly an interesting legend, Mother. I enjoyed it ever so much. I do wish that I could pick up one of those Indian arrows though, for my collection. That would just be perfect."

Mrs. Geary smiled down at his earnest face. "I don't believe that you'll find any here, dear. The

mouth of the cave has been widened and the rocks carried away. Visitors have also carried away all the curios. But the cave and the legends still remain the same throughout the years.

"But come now. We have almost a sixty-mile drive back to Aunt Grace's in Burns, and we have stayed here much longer than we had planned."

Mr. and Mrs. Geary walked on to the car, but Edwin stood at the cave entrance, looking back toward the cavern, dreaming of the days when it was peopled with dusky-skinned, black-eyed figures.

They had walked up and down this very trail and called out to one another and laughed. Within these very walls their war cry had echoed.

A low hum filled the air. Edwin jumped. Then a smile lighted his face.

"I almost thought I really heard the Paiutes," he cried as he ran toward his parents. "And then I knew it was only the car engine starting."

He turned for a last look and waved his hat as they drove away. "Good-by, Malheur Cave, Good-by."

10

Cecil's Hill Crash

BUT YOU promised, Mother," wailed Gwendolen. Hot tears filled her eyes as she rubbed the frosted windowpane and stared blindly out across the snow-filled valley.

"You promised that I could go coasting on Cecil's Hill with Hal and Hazel, and I've been counting on it for days and days. Next week we'll have to go back to school, and then there won't be any time for play—hardly any, at least."

"Yes, dear, I know," sighed mother patiently. "I really did promise that you could go to Cecil's Hill with the Hibbard children, but that was before you were ill in bed with a severe cold. Sometimes it is best not to hold one to a promise when circumstances have changed previously made plans."

"But I'm well enough now," teased Gwendolen. "After all, I've been up and around the house since Monday, and I feel just fine. O Mother, I can hardly wait to try out the new sled that grandpa gave me. Please, please let me go."

Mrs. Lampshire put her arm around her daughter and kissed the soft young cheek, looking at her intently before she spoke.

"Since you are almost well, and since I did promise, I am going to let you go———"

"O Mother, thank you. Thank you!" interrupted Gwendolen, twirling round and round in her excitement, her wool dress flaring out over her black-stockinged legs.

"Just a moment, dear," mother added. "I hadn't quite finished. It is because you have been an obedient girl that I am giving you permission, and there are two requests that I am going to ask you to obey. The first is that you must not be gone longer than one hour, and the second is that you must not take more than two long slides down Cecil's Hill road.

"The air is very cold, even though the sun is shining, and as an onlooker you are likely soon to be chilled through. Besides this, Mrs. Hibbard told me today that the hill is very icy. All the neighborhood children have been carrying buckets of water from the pump in Mr. Cecil's yard and pouring it on the sidewalk. By now the water has frozen into a solid sheet of ice. Your new sled with its sharp runners will travel like lightning. I know that you are not yet strong enough to steer it safely past the telephone pole at the bottom of the steep sidewalk runway. Be sure to stay out in the middle of the main road, away from the narrow footpath. You'll find the road itself quite smooth enough for good coasting."

"Hello! We're ready," called Hazel from the big bare

poplar tree by the front gate. As soon as Gwendolen opened the door she continued, her breath rising like a white cloud in the bitterly cold air, "Hal's coming in just a minute and then we're going around the block to get Burns McGowan and Frances and Teresa. Next we'll go past Dr. Geary's and get Woodbridge too.

"Be sure to wrap up good and warm. It's awfully cold. I'll go on over to Donegan's, and you can come along with Hal." She beat her mittened hands together before she hurried down the snow-encrusted walk, her old homemade sled dragging at her heels.

Gwendolen hurried into her warm winter coat as she heard Hal's shrill whistle. She fastened the heavy black galoshes and pulled on her red hand-knit tassel cap and mittens. Then she gave her mother a hasty kiss, grabbed the new sled at the edge of the steps, and, with Hal, hurried toward the group of children waiting impatiently at the corner.

"Oh, good!" cried Hazel. "I was really afraid that your mother'd make you stay at home today. We wouldn't have had nearly so much fun without you." Hazel's sky-blue eyes flashed joyfully as she spied the new red-and-yellow sled.

"Look at that beautiful red Flyer! Aren't you a lucky girl, though! I can barely wait to see how fast it'll go. I'm anxious to see you try it on the icy footpath on Cecil's Hill. You'll be sure to win over everyone else."

"You've got to win," nodded Teresa. "We've planned a race with the eighth graders, and our seventh grade has just got to win."

"I—I guess I could win, all right." Gwendolen's

heart sank as she saw her playmates' eager faces looking directly at her. "But—well, you see, mother doesn't want me to go down the footpath today. She says it's dangerous when covered with so much ice. She's afraid that I might have an accident."

"Oh, pooh!" scoffed Burns, tossing his red head defiantly. "There's ab-so-lutely nothing to be afraid of. Ab-so-lutely nothing. Why, there's a high stone wall all along one side, so you couldn't slide off the path if you wanted to. And any sissy could steer clear of that pole at the bottom. You can see it ahead of you for two blocks before you get there."

He stopped and eyed her curiously before he continued. "Besides, you've gone down that path hundreds of times and nothing's ever happened to you. Don't tell me you're getting to be a fraidy cat." He shrugged his plump shoulders and eyed her scornfully.

Gwendolen's cheeks burned and her throat ached with the unkind words that she longed to answer. But instead she trudged along in silence as her playmates hurried ahead to the top of the hill.

"Hurry up, everybody. We're almost ready to start." Happy greetings and gay laughter filled the wintry air as several dozen schoolmates gathered in an excited huddle to plan the order of racing. Gwendolen stood on the outside of the circle, where she could get a closer look at the long, steep slope of the narrow, frozen footpath. How smooth and glassy it looked with its clear ice crust gleaming in the sunlight. Sharp little tingles ran up and down her spine as she imagined the wonderful feel of the rushing wind on that swooping plunge and the breathtaking coldness of the spraying ice crystals as they blew across her bare face.

She stood there, thinking how she would love to coast down that steep slope!

She cast a disdainful glance at the wide road beyond. Flying figures on gaily painted sleds darted like swallows down its hard-packed snow and toiled antlike up its steep slope. Gwendolen thought that it might be fun to coast there *if* the forbidden footpath were not so temptingly near.

"Come on. Let's go down, just for practice, before the races begin," called a voice right in her ear. She jumped as she turned around and looked into Frances' cheerful, rosy face.

"I can't go down the path today," she said slowly. "And mother told me not to go down the road more than two times. She's afraid I'm still rather weak after being in bed so long."

"You look all right to me," Frances answered, looking critically at her friend. "You've got just as many freckles as ever, although they do look a little paler. Well, it's too bad, but it can't be helped. Your mother always means just what she says, and if you disobey, I know you won't be allowed to coast for ever so long. But it is a shame! Those old eighth graders are sure to win if you don't help our side, and they'll never let us forget it, either. We'd counted on your new sled today." She sighed as she walked slowly toward June and Mildred.

Gwendolen's heart sank with disappointment. So bitter were her angry thoughts that she scarcely heard the loud, excited cries of "Go. Hurry. Faster. Rah! Rah! Rah! for the eighth grade," as, one by one, the older students flew like snowbirds downward to victory, finishing a few inches ahead of the out-distanced seventh graders.

The creeping cold and her classmates' cries for revenge startled her into action. "I might as well take my first turn," she thought, "before I get too cold to move. My hour must be nearly up, so I might as well have a little fun while I can."

She pulled her sled over to the top of the roadway and, lying flat along its shiny untried surface, started down, side by side with Regina, one of the eighth-grade contestants.

"Rah! Rah! Rah! for our side. Three cheers! We won," shouted the joyous seventh-grade onlookers from the hilltop, gleefully dancing up and down.

"Good for you, Gwendolen. Try it again. Maybe we've still got a chance to win," Burns shouted loudly through his cupped hands.

"9 to 6. Isn't that the score?" asked Woodbridge anxiously as he shivered in the sharp December wind. "Oh, if we could only make four points we'd be ahead."

"That's right, we would," added Hal. "And think how much fun it would be to go back to school as the Cecil's Hill winners. We'd show those smart eighth graders that we can outrace them. But it looks pretty hopeless right now."

As Gwendolen pulled her Flyer to the very top of the hill her excited companions rushed toward her and urged her to race again. Without stopping to think about the unaccustomed pounding in her chest or the unusual shortness of her breath, she again flung herself upon the beautiful new coaster. Three more times she swept down the hill to victory, and three more times she climbed the hill with her friends' cries ringing sweetly in her humming ears. But now her knees wobbled slightly, and she gratefully sank down on the sled's smooth surface to rest.

"We're winning. We're winning," cried Hazel. "You beat Frank Loggan last time, and now it's a tie. 9 to 9. O Gwendolen, you've got to go once more. You can do better than any of us, and we've just *got* to win."

"Come on," yelled Hal. "We've decided to run the last race on the footpath. It's wide enough for two sleds and it's as slick as glass. This race'll really be exciting."

Gwendolen had felt pleasantly warmed by her classmates' praise and by the excitement of the race. She jumped quickly to her feet only to stop short. For the very first time since entering the contest she remembered her mother's warning. "I want you to take only two slides down the hill. Stay out in the middle of the main road. I know that you're not strong enough yet to steer your sled down the narrow footpath."

Suddenly the warm, pleasant glow left her, and she felt pale and cold. She half opened her lips to say, "But I can't coast on the footpath. I promised mother that I wouldn't. And I've already coasted down more times than I'm allowed to do today."

But somehow the words stuck in her throat, and try as she might she could not say them. Mutely she pulled her Flyer over to the top of the footpath and waited for her opponent to reach the starting line. As in a dream she heard her classmates shout, "Go on, Gwendolen.

You've got to win. You've just got to!" As in a dream she heard the eighth grade cheer wildly for Frank Loggan.

Then without stopping to listen further to that disturbing little inner voice Gwendolen flung herself upon her sled. She stared straight ahead as the steel runners began to bite sharply into the sparkling surface. How narrow and steep the path suddenly became. She shook her dizzy head as the Flyer gathered momentum and sped faster and faster beside the high stone fence. She stared anxiously ahead, blinking her dazzled eyes in a vain attempt to banish the black specks that floated strangely in front of her. Swallowlike she swooped down over the sparkling crystals, her sled runners cutting crisply along the dangerous, glassy path.

Closer and closer and closer she rushed toward the huge telephone pole at the end of the runway. It loomed larger and larger before her frightened eyes. Her heart leaped as the object seemed to move directly into her pathway. Gwendolen's mittened hands tried frantically to tighten their grasp upon the steering bar, but all her efforts were in vain. Her arms felt cold and limp and lifeless as her hands clung numbly to the now unguided sled careening wildly out of control.

Thirty feet, twenty feet, ten feet—then with a sickening thud she crashed head-on into the immovable telephone pole at the foot of Cecil's Hill.

Gwendolen felt one sharp blow before she sank down, down into a thick, smothering blackness that rolled up and around her until the sun and daylight were completely blotted out and she knew nothing more.

A hoarse rasping noise that intermingled strangely

with frightened voices sounded in Gwendolen's ears as she struggled back to consciousness. But it was several moments before she realized that the rough noise was her own painful, labored breathing. She tried to move, only to wince in pain at the slight effort.

"Here. Don't move. We'll lift you onto my sled and pull you home," Hazel said sympathetically as she knelt down and rubbed Gwendolen's forehead with a handful of snow.

"Oooooooh! Ouch!" moaned the unfortunate victim. "Wh—what——"

"Don't try to talk," warned Hal. "You crashed head-on into the big telephone pole, and it knocked you breathless. You've got a bump the size of a goose egg on your head and a cut on your arm, but I really don't think any bones are broken. We'll hurry and get you home, though, if you think you can stand being moved. I expect your mother'll want to call Dr. Geary."

Gwendolen never forgot the agony of that bumpy, jolting ride over the ridges of hard-frozen snow in the rutted road. Every jar sent a sharp, knifelike pain through her bruised head and bleeding arm. And the sight of Burns carrying the sad remaining sticks of her once-beautiful new Flyer was almost more than she could bear.

It seemed an hour before the sad little procession turned in at the front gate to be met by white-faced Mrs. Lampshire. It seemed another hour before she was at last tucked safely into her warm, comfortable bed, with mother hovering sympathetically near while kind Dr. Geary looked at her bandaged arm and gave her a sedative. She was just drifting off to sleep when she heard the doctor speak to mother.

"Well, from what Woodbridge told me, I guess this girl of yours won the Cecil's Hill coasting championship for the seventh grade. He said that she was a full sled length ahead in crossing the goal line just before she crashed. Too bad the new sled's ruined, though. Her injuries will soon heal, but that sled's damaged beyond repair. I took a look at it as I came in, and there's nothing left but kindling wood."

Gwendolen's heavy eyes opened slowly and looked waveringly into mother's sorrowful face. Though her tongue felt strangely thick and it was an effort to talk, she felt that she *must* speak to mother.

"It—it served me right, Mother," she whispered shakily. "You knew best after all! I just wasn't strong enough to steer away from danger, and I deserved my punishment. Winning that contest for the seventh grade wasn't at all important compared to disobeying you and ruining my beautiful sled. Next time I'll know better than to hold you to a promise."

11

Violin in the Sage

GWENDOLEN LOOKED out of the window just in time to see her very best friend hurrying along the sun-baked road toward the Lampshire house.

"Mother, June's coming," she called. "May I go back home with her if she invites me?"

A flushed, smiling mother stepped through the kitchen doorway. She had already started the noonday meal. The good smell of roast and dressing and lemon pies drifted into the cool, darkened living room. As she smoothed down her crisp blue gingham apron she shook her head.

"No, dear, I'm afraid not. You girls may visit for a little while. But as soon as June leaves, you must do your practicing."

Gwendolen's lower lip pouted out into what her father called a "regular chicken roost."

"Oh, please, Mother," she begged. "Since school was out we've had hardly any time to really play. And now that the big yellow rose bush near Dalton's front windows is in bloom we can play house in its shade. We'd have such a good time. Please, please, let me go. I'll practice my whole hour when I come back. Honestly I will."

But when mother shook her head, Gwendolen did not say another word. She knew that coaxing would do no good. Only the week before, they had had what mother called a "session." It was right after she had trudged the long, hot two miles home from her violin lesson at Mrs. Dodge's. She found that she had forgotten to put her bow in the violin case. Mother had made her turn right around and go back to her teacher's for the forgotten bow.

"You are old enough to know that you must work very hard. Right now you have a chance to study with a good violin teacher." Mother had put her arm around Gwendolen's waist and kissed her cheek.

"Our little town of Burns is very fortunate to have a fine music teacher. Mrs. Dodge has studied and taught in Boston, New York, and Paris," said her mother. "It is only because she is the bride of a young civil engineer that she has come so far away from these large cities. If her husband has to work somewhere else she will leave this place.

"You must make the most of your chance. Practice hard every day. Daddy and I hope that you will be a good violinist. Perhaps someday you will play before governors or even kings and queens. Your grandfather did, you know. He played the cornet in the queen's band in England."

Gwendolen's mind had buzzed with angry thoughts as she retraced her weary steps to Mrs. Dodge's home near the Robin Hood swimming hole in Silvies River.

"I'm almost sorry I ever heard the Burns Sagebrush Orchestra play," she grumbled. She kicked angrily at the tall weed border along the plank sidewalk.

"It was right after their concert that I begged and begged dad and mother to get me a violin. They sent for the one that Grandpa Linton used to play. I never thought about the long hours I'd have to practice on it before I could be in the orchestra!"

At a rap on the door Gwendolen ran quickly to greet June. She was anxious to tell her good news to her friend. She knew that her playmate would be glad, for she was never selfish or unkind or cross.

"Oh, June," she cried excitedly as she hugged the dark-haired girl. "Guess what! I'll give you three guesses."

June's brown eyes laughed merrily. "I need just *one* guess. You're really a member of the Sagebrush Orchestra now. And you'll play in the orchestra concert in Tona-wama Hall next month!"

Gwendolen again hugged her chum before she let go and jumped gleefully up and down on the thick Brussels carpet.

"Isn't it wonderful? Just think. I've been studying violin only a few months. But already I can play well enough to be in the first big concert! I'm in the octet, too," she added importantly.

"Honestly?" June asked with breathless interest. "Who's in it? Is Agnes Foley playing? Isn't she one of the best players—she and Kathleen?"

"No, Agnes is going away to school this fall. And

Kathleen plays some solos. I'm first. Then come Hazel, Gladys, Rozelle, Frances, Katherine, Margaret, and Jessie. I'm the tallest of the eight girls. That's why I'm first in line.

"We're going to play 'Marche Militaire' from memory. And we're all going to wear new white dresses and big white satin hair ribbons and white stockings. The other girls will have white shoes, too. But mother says my new black pumps will have to do. Little Stephanie needs new shoes right away—she grows out of everything so fast."

"Well, you're a lucky girl," spoke June wistfully. "If I could take music lessons, I'd certainly be happy. I don't know that I would do so well as a violinist. I'd really rather learn to play the piano. But I'd certainly love to hear all those records that Mrs. Dodge plays for her pupils. Didn't you say you'd heard all the great artists on her phonograph?"

"Yes, I have," nodded Gwendolen. "Mrs. Dodge always lets me choose a record after my lesson. She tells me about each musician, too. I like all of them ever so much. But I especially like Mischa Elman, Madame Schumann-Heink, and Fritz Kreisler."

"Are they all violinists?" questioned June. "I thought that Madame Schumann-Heink was a singer. We studied about her in school. She was born in Germany."

"Yes, she's a very great singer," nodded Gwendolen. "We don't listen to just violin solos. Every week after our regular orchestra practice Mrs. Dodge plays all kinds of records for us. Then sometimes we go for a swim in Robin Hood pool. Mrs. Dodge taught me how to swim there. Or sometimes we have a tea party after our orchestra practice.

"Oh, it's lots of fun," she said, forgetting how she had grumbled about her practicing. "I just love Mrs. Dodge. She's so good and kind, and she knows *everything* about music."

"Well, you're a lucky girl to get to take lessons," sighed June. "That's all I can say. I'll certainly be at the concert to clap for you."

It was lots of fun to visit with June. The older girl rested for a while before returning home with some silverware Mrs. Dalton had borrowed for the Mothers' Club meeting that afternoon.

But it was not so much fun to go back into the cool, darkened living room, take out the old violin, and begin to practice scales and chords.

"Keep right on," called mother from the kitchen, as the young violinist stopped to glance at the tall mantel clock. "How long have you practiced?"

"Just fifteen minutes," wailed Gwendolen. "And that leaves forty-five minutes more."

However, she really did have a good feeling clear down inside when she at last carefully wrapped the shining instrument in its silk handkerchief covering and put it away in the purple-lined leather case. Now that she had worked on her studies and had finished memorizing another line of the march she could play games for the rest of the morning.

She ran across the wide vine-shaded screened porch, down the broad front steps, and out onto the clover lawn. Two hummingbirds darted back and forth among the gaily colored morning-glories and nasturtiums. Several bright-hued butterflies fluttered across the fence to the Hibbard yard next door.

"Come on over," called Hazel. "Frances Donegan just came. We'll play croquet for a while."

The happy hour of play, dinnertime, and the afternoon rest period passed quickly. At four o'clock Gwendolen hurried to Tonawama Hall for an orchestra rehearsal. She had just finished tuning her violin when Mrs. Dodge clapped her hands and motioned for everyone to be quiet.

"Children, we must practice hard," she said. "We have been asked to ride in a very lovely float in the Fourth of July parade next month. Not only that, but we have been asked to give our concert the night of the Fourth. I can't tell you any more now. But please remember that we must do our very best. There may be a wonderful surprise for all of you if you play well."

"What do you suppose it can be?" Gwendolen whispered to Miriam.

"I don't know," softly answered Miriam. "But I am sure that it'll be something worth while. You know that Mrs. Dodge never breaks a promise."

Although the late afternoon was very warm, the children practiced faithfully. During that month they met each weekday afternoon in the hot, stuffy hall and played from memory all their orchestra numbers.

The morning of the Fourth was clear and sunny. Gwendolen carefully dipped warm water from the reservoir on the side of the kitchen range and partly filled the round tin tub for her bath. She felt fresh and clean as she dressed. She carefully put on her long white stockings and black patent leather pumps and slipped into her pretty white dress with its puffed sleeves and ribbon sash.

"I wonder what the surprise will be," she asked eagerly, as mother tied wide white satin hair ribbons on her long yellow curls.

"I think you'll have to wait until tonight to find out," smiled mother. "It will depend on how well you and the other children play at the concert.

"But run along now. Here is your violin case. One surprise is waiting for you down by daddy's garage. The orchestra is to meet there for the parade. Be very careful of your dress. As soon as you come home be sure to take it off. You must keep it fresh-looking for tonight's concert, you know."

Gwendolen's legs fairly twinkled as she hurried over the hilltop and down the slope to Lampshire's garage. As she rounded the corner she gasped and stopped dead still. She almost rubbed her eyes to see if she were dreaming.

For there, in the middle of the street, stood a violin.

It was a huge violin. Gwendolen thought that surely it must be the grandfather of all violins. It was shaped exactly right. It had four large ropes stretched down its middle, for strings, and it had an enormous bow which was held in place by a pretty girl orchestra member.

The great violin lay flat on a big wooden float whose lower part was covered by white cloth printed with the words and music of "My Country 'Tis of Thee." And the hollow inner part of the instrument was filled with excited boys and girls, members of the Sagebrush Orchestra.

"Come on," called Katherine and Frank, as they caught sight of her. "Hurry up and climb in. We'll soon be ready to start!"

What fun it was to stand in the slowly moving violin float and play an orchestra number directed by five-year-old Katherine. Among the friendly, smiling faces in the crowd she saw those of her own folks: dad, mother, and little sister Stephanie, Grandma Linton, Uncle Roy, and Aunt Jessie. The Hibbards, Frances, and June waved to her and smiled broadly.

"Rest awhile, children," finally called Mrs. Dodge. "We are going on to the edge of town. Our driver will take us out into the sagebrush, where our picture will be taken. This picture will be printed in the Portland papers for thousands of people in the Pacific Northwest to see."

Gwendolen and her orchestra friends looked at each other with round, astonished eyes. Portland! Why, Portland was the largest city in the State of Oregon. It was hundreds of miles from the little town of Burns. The nearest railroad leading to the "City of Roses" was at Bend, 150 miles across the flat, dusty, sagebrush-covered desert. They could hardly realize that people in Portland would see them pictured on their violin float!

After the pictures were taken, they returned to the garage and met their families. When the Lampshires went home for a quick lunch on the cool porch, Gwendolen hurried up to her dainty pink-and-blue bedroom. She took off her new white dress and carefully hung it in the big closet. She washed her face and hands in the flowered china washbowl. Then she slipped into a soft pongee dress and hurried back downstairs.

The hours sped by. Suddenly it was evening and concerttime. Gwendolen listened carefully to the A pitch that Mrs. Dodge sounded with her own violin. When she had tuned the A string she carefully tuned her three other strings. Then she listened to each one until they were just right: E-A-D-G. Mrs. Dodge and Signor Meriggioli listened to each instrument to be sure that it was in tune.

"There is noth-i-ing wor-r-rse sounding in all the world than an instrument out of tune," said Signor Meriggioli. "It makes my ears to hur-r-rt!" He smiled at Gwendolen, and she smiled back at Mr. "Merry-jolly." She liked the little brown flutist, who had helped Mrs. Dodge with their orchestra. Mrs. Dodge had told them that he was a graduate of the famous Milan, Italy, music conservatory and a very fine flute player. Gwendolen loved to listen to the clear, beautiful tones pouring from the small silver instrument held up to Mr. "Merry-jolly's" lips.

With a last whispered word Mrs. Dodge gave the signal. The curtain rose on the group of young boys and girls playing Luders' "The Prince of Pilsen."

Number after number followed, all played from memory. The audience clapped loudly after each piece. At last it was time for the octet to play. Gwendolen's knees trembled as she stood near the stage entrance at the head of the line of eight girls.

"Let's hear your A again, girls," whispered Mrs. Dodge. "Tune your E string a little higher, Gladys, and your D string a little lower, Gwendolen. Now you're ready. Hold your violins up and get a nice, big tone. Don't forget to bow when you have finished."

For a few moments after the start of Schubert's "Marche Militaire" Gwendolen could see only a blur of faces down in front of her. She had not thought that she would be frightened, but she was. However, as the round, full tones of the singing strings rang out, her knees stopped trembling. The blur before her eyes cleared away.

And there, right down on the front seat, smiling up as she had promised to do, was June.

Gwendolen's bow was even firmer and her notes even stronger from that time on. And when the audience clapped so hard that the octet had to go back and repeat their number, she decided that it was really fun to be able to play for others.

Gwendolen had just started to put away her violin at the end of the concert when Mrs. Dodge hurried smilingly toward them.

"We're ready for the surprise," she said in a low voice. "Go quietly down the side stairs and take the seats which have been saved for you."

"I've been wondering all evening about our surprise.

Haven't you?" Gwendolen whispered to Hazel. "Do you suppose it's something to eat?"

"Maybe so," nodded Hazel. "It might be pink lemonade and popcorn. I'd like that!"

"Why, it's Colonel Bill Hanley, from the Double-O Ranch," said Gwendolen, as she sank into a seat next to June. "What do you suppose he's doing up on the stage? He's handing something to the mayor of Burns. What *can* it be?"

"S-sh! Listen and find out," laughed June.

"I have been asked to make an announcement to the Sagebrush Orchestra." The mayor cleared his throat and began to speak.

"Colonel Hanley, a number of the orchestra members, parents, and some of the Burns business firms have pledged $2,000. This money will be used for the Sagebrush Orchestra. These children and their teacher and director, Mrs. Mary V. Dodge, have been given a great honor. They have been invited to spend a week in Portland and Salem.

"In the City of Roses they have been invited by Phil Metschan, Jr., of the Imperial Hotel, to be his guests. They will play several programs while in the Rose City. They will be entertained by many clubs. They will see many interesting sights.

"In Salem, which is the capital of Oregon, the orchestra will play at the Oregon State Fair. We think that they may even win a prize at the fair.

"They will have a wonderful trip, and we are glad. We are very proud of Mrs. Dodge and of our young musicians of Harney County."

Thrills ran up and down Gwendolen's back as she heard the mayor's speech. She squeezed June's hand as everyone cheered and Mrs. Dodge came out and bowed to the audience.

"Isn't it wonderful?" she cried. "Just think! We'll get to travel on the train and stay in a real hotel. I've done both, but most of the orchestra members haven't. Most of them haven't even *seen* a train."

"I'm awfully glad for you," said June. She smiled at her friend. "I think that you've had a real surprise. It was certainly worth working for. It won't be half so hard to practice from now on."

Gwendolen looked at June. "Oh, June," she cried. "I've been so glad over my own good luck that I'd forgotten you couldn't go along. I wish you belonged to our orchestra."

"Don't worry about me!" smiled June. "When my folks saw that big violin float in today's parade they decided to give me a chance to study music. Only I'm going to take piano lessons. Then later on I can play your accompaniments. Won't that be fun?"

The two little girls joyfully hugged each other as Gwendolen exclaimed, "It's just like a dream come true. Let's go tell Mrs. Dodge. After all, we owe all our good luck to her and to her *Violin in the Sage*."

12

Birthday on Wheels

"OH, I WISH I could go out to the gym too. Because I have to sit here at my desk I *always* miss all the recess periods and the assembly programs." Sharon's blue eyes filled with hot tears that burned against her eyelids. But as she looked at Stephen she tried to smile bravely.

"Say, I'm sorry. Really I am, Sharon. And so are all the rest of your classmates," Stephen answered quickly. "We'd certainly like to have you there in the gym with the rest of us. We'd carry you down the steps if we could, but Mrs. Mosser said we might drop you. And that would be dangerous. We wouldn't want you to get hurt."

Sharon felt her schoolmate's gaze upon the heavy iron braces and even heavier shoes that she herself wore each day to school. Her own eyes rested upon the crutches that were her constant companions and without whose aid she could not walk.

"If I only had a wheel chair I could learn to get around almost as fast as the rest of you," Sharon replied thoughtfully. "But—well, that's out of the question. I know daddy just can't afford to get one for me, much as he'd like to. Everything costs so much that it's all the folks can do to buy food and clothing for all six of us. Daddy works awfully hard but there's never enough money left over for a wheel chair."

R-r-r-r-r-r-r-r-ing!

"There's the afternoon bell for classes to begin. For once I'm here on time," chuckled Stephen. "Guess it was a good thing I came in to talk to you, Sharon."

Stephen's brown eyes twinkled merrily as he looked at the flushed, breathless sixth graders who ran hurriedly to their seats. S-E-C-R-E-T his glance spelled to Don, Judith, Muriel, Ora Lee, Lynette, Beverly, and Nancy. S-E-C-R-E-T, answered their knowing nods as they sat down and opened their spelling books for their first afternoon class period.

Sharon felt the hour speed by, for spelling was one of her favorite subjects. But to her impatient fifth and sixth grade classmates that one hour dragged by with all the slowness of the fabled tortoise who raced the hare.

Bong! Bong!

Stephen and his classmates jumped as the big wall clock struck the hour.

"It's two o'clock," whispered Stephen to Don. "I thought the hands on that old thing would never move around. And then they got there when I least expected them to."

"That's exactly the way I feel too," replied Don.

"I can hardly wait," murmured Lynette. "Is Mrs. Howell here yet?"

"Sh-h-h!" warned Ora Lee. "Sharon'll hear you. That would spoil everything."

Fifth and sixth grade boys and girls sat up straight as their teacher turned from the blackboard and smiled at them. Their eyes looked toward Sharon as Mrs. Mosser began to speak.

"Today we are going to have a special assembly. I'm sure that we'll all enjoy the occasion very much. However, instead of going out to the auditorium we'll go downstairs to the dining hall."

"Oh, good," exclaimed Sharon. "Maybe I'll get to go for once. I've never yet been to an assembly."

"That's right, Sharon. You *are* going to attend this program," nodded Mrs. Mosser, smiling at her most studious pupil. "I hear our principal's footsteps coming down the hall right now. He and Mr. Anderson are going to carry you down the stairs. Then we'll begin our program."

"All ready, boys and girls. March quietly, so you won't disturb the upper grades. After all, only the first six grades are invited to this special affair. Since there isn't room for everyone downstairs we had to limit our invitations."

"What kind of program are we going to have, Mr. Baker?" Sharon asked quickly, as the school principal carefully lifted her small body encased in its heavy iron braces. She laughed out loud as her blond curls bounced across his nose and almost caused him to sneeze.

"You'll have to ask Mrs. Mosser," answered Mr.

Baker. "I'm not in charge of today's assembly program. But I'm sure you'll enjoy what has been planned."

"Oh, I know I will," Sharon said earnestly. "It's a real treat for me to be here."

Stephen and Don grinned slyly at each other as Mr. Baker and Mr. Anderson entered the dining hall and carefully lowered Sharon into a chair in the middle of the front row. They saw the girls bite their lips to keep from laughing aloud as Mrs. Mosser and Mrs. Howell entered the room and walked to a gaily decorated table upon which were spread a number of cards and prettily wrapped packages.

"Why, there's our Sabbath school teacher!" exclaimed Sharon to her companions. "How nice that she's visiting us just now. But I wonder how she happened to come today? Maybe she's planning something extra special for our Investment program for the boys and girls in foreign lands. Maybe——"

"Happy birthday to you——" interrupted the joyous voices of her schoolmates. Sharon gasped with amazement and looked wonderingly from them to her smiling teacher and to Mrs. Howell.

"Happy birthday, dear Sharon, happy birthday to you."

"To—to me?" Sharon choked, trying to swallow hard against the big lump that seemed almost to fill her throat. "You—you mean you knew this was my birthday? But—but how——" Her voice faltered and trailed away into the silence that fell upon the room as Mrs. Mosser spoke.

"You see, Sharon, Mrs. Howell is here for a special

reason. She was the one who first learned about your twelfth birthday, and she was the one who came and talked to us about planning this surprise for you. You have been a good and faithful student in Eugene Junior Academy, and by your cheerful ways and your happy and ready smile you have done much to make our schoolroom a pleasant place.

"You have proved to all of us that greatness of spirit is not measured by physical health. It has been a privilege for all of us to make this birthday an especially happy one for you."

"Oh, Mrs. Mosser," Sharon began. But her unfinished sentence was lost in the big OOOOOOOOOOH that followed Shirley Moon's entrance into the room, proudly carrying the big pink and white cake baked especially for this gala occasion.

"For—for me?" Sharon exclaimed time and again, as she opened the many birthday cards and the many nice gifts that had been brought to the school not only by classmates but by interested townspeople as well. Especially noticed was the large supply of colored pencils, paints, and art supplies given by the Graves Music and Art Store.

"I—I just love them all," Sharon said softly. "I can't thank you enough for all you've done. Why, it's been such a surprise I'm all out of breath."

"Then you'd better inhale a fresh supply of air right now," joked Stephen. "The best is yet to come."

"You mean there's *more?*" gasped Sharon. "Why what more could any girl want than all these gifts and that wonderful cake and the green ice cream and——"

"Oh, Oh, OH!" cried Sharon. As several of her classmates walked toward her she reached forward with eager hands. "A wheel chair! It's a wheel chair! At last I'll be able to go out on the playground with all of you. I can go to programs in the gymnasium too. And I can go to all the church programs, even when daddy isn't there to carry me down the long hallways and aisles.

"How wonderful this is. Thank you, everyone. I can hardly wait to show daddy and mother. Won't they be surprised and glad?"

Sharon's smiling, tear-wet eyes looked toward her classmates and teachers, and her hands tightened upon the wheels of the shining new chrome and leather chair as she lowered herself into the soft seat.

"I don't think I can ever be surprised again," she concluded. "Today has been just one big surprise after another. And this is the best one of all."

But Sharon found that she and all her classmates had one more surprise in store for them a few evenings later when she picked up the afternoon edition of the Eugene *Register-Guard.*

"Why, Mother. Look!" Sharon called as she turned to page 7A. "Here's a picture of me in my wheel chair with my sixth-grade classmates standing around me. And right underneath the picture is a story about my surprise birthday party. It's written by Stephen's mother.

"Why, I didn't know that the photographer who came to school was going to put this picture in the paper. I didn't suppose that anyone would be interested in me. After all, I can't walk fast or run or do lots of things that my friends can do."

Sharon felt her mother's soft arms around her and her mother's kiss on the top of her beautiful curls. Then she heard her mother's kind voice as she answered:

"Never forget, Sharon, that every person has been given one or more talents to use for good. One person may be given the talent of good health and a strong body. Another may be given the talent of a keen mind and a sunny disposition. Still another may possess all of these.

"Although you have been denied a strong body, you have been blessed with a keen mind. You also have been blessed with a cheerful disposition, which can bring much happiness to others around you if you will but let your light shine. You can see that you are fortunate to have two talents instead of only one.

"Just think of George Hibbard, whose stories you have so much enjoyed. For more than twenty years he has been totally paralyzed from the neck down. Yet so great has been his courage and his unselfish interest in others that hundreds go to see him and to receive encouragement from him.

"Remember, too, that others who read this story may be impressed to do equally helpful deeds for the many handicapped people who live close to them. There are many folks who need help. I think the newspaper story will sum up very well both your happy birthday and this thought of helping others.

"Now take the paper and start reading aloud. Daddy and the boys and I will listen closely to every word."

New Wheel Chair Makes Birthday Happy

Smiles triumphed over tears when Sharon Tison cele-
brated her 12th birthday at Eugene Junior Academy on
April 15. When Sharon left home that morning, proudly
wearing the new blue dress her mother had just finished
making, she knew nothing of the exciting hour scheduled
for 2 p.m. in the school dining room. Even when her
sixth grade teacher, Mrs. Robert Mosser, announced a
special class assembly and the little girl had been carried
downstairs, Sharon still had no suspicion that she was the
guest of honor. Not until her classmates began to sing
"Happy Birthday" did she realize that all the birthday
cards and gifts were really for her, as well as the big
pink and white cake presented by Shirley Moon and a
large serving of green ice cream brought by Mrs. Ed
Howell.

But the best surprise was reserved until last. That
was when smiles triumphed over joyful tears, for there
stood the long-dreamed-of but vainly-hoped-for wheel
chair that Sharon has needed in order to attend school
assemblies in the gymnasium and to be with her classmates on the playground. "Oh," she exclaimed breathlessly, "now I can go places just like the rest of you.
Now I won't have to sit in the schoolroom all the time!"

Sharon's first two years' schoolwork was done in
Bend, where a visiting teacher helped her four hours
weekly. Grades three and four were done under the
supervision of the Eugene School for Crippled Children,
where she progressed sufficiently to transfer to Eugene
Junior Academy for grades five and six. Sharon's sunny
disposition and friendliness have made her a favorite
among her classmates but her heavy braces and shoes and

her ever-present crutches have confined her to her desk.

The new chair will be kept at school during the week but will be taken home each weekend, when Sharon will have more time to experiment in its use.

Each year Eugene Junior Academy school children have a church Investment Program, at which time they bring in the money they have earned for Seventh-day Adventist Foreign Missions. This year, in addition to this work, the children of the first six grades, under the sponsorship of Mrs. Howell, also have invested in the happiness of one of their own classmates.

Sharon's happiness was reflected in the faces of her classmates as they clustered around her. Sharon herself is convinced that Investment Day and Happy Birthday are for her one and the same.